THE NEW RYTHUM
AND OTHER PIECES

RONALD FIRBANK
photographed by Elliott and Fry in 1917

THE NEW RYTHUM
AND OTHER PIECES

by

RONALD FIRBANK

GERALD DUCKWORTH & CO. LTD.
3 Henrietta Street, London, W.C.2

First Published 1962

© THOMAS FIRBANK 1962

INTRODUCTION © GERALD DUCKWORTH & CO. LTD. 1962

PRINTED IN GREAT BRITAIN
BY EBENEZER BAYLIS AND SON, LTD.
THE TRINITY PRESS, WORCESTER, AND LONDON

CONTENTS

LIST OF ILLUSTRATIONS

*Photographs not otherwise acknowledged are
reproduced here by courtesy of Thomas Firbank*

INTRODUCTION

BY ALAN HARRIS

IN 1930, four years after Ronald Firbank's death, Mr
Kyrle Fletcher's *Memoir*, which all subsequent writers on
Firbank can only gratefully pillage, revealed that he had
been engaged at the time of his death on a novel set in
New York and that the ten years between *Odette d'Antrevernes* & *A Study in Temperament* (1905) and *Vainglory*
(1915), in which he published nothing, had not been
completely unproductive; but he was able to tell us
virtually nothing about the novel, and about the unpublished writings only the little he had gathered from
examining two typescripts that had found their way into
an antiquarian bookseller's shop. A year or two afterwards the late Sir Coleridge Kennard, who had been a
friend of Firbank's youth, produced the manuscript of a
complete unpublished novel, *The Artificial Princess*, which
was published in 1934 and at once took its place with the
other novels. It was, as Kennard called it, 'a mature and
typical work', and could therefore confidently be dated
not much before *Vainglory*. That it saw the light when it
did was entirely due to the fact that Firbank, shortly before his death, had second thoughts about publication and
consulted the late Lord Berners, in whose hands the
manuscript was when he died. Lord Berners kept it for
a time and then handed it over to Kennard.

The rest of Firbank's papers passed into the keeping

of his sister Heather, and remained there, along with other family papers and the hoarded dresses of her youth, until her death in 1951, when her heir, Lieutenant-Colonel Thomas Firbank, found himself the owner of fifty-odd trunks and boxes in store at the Pantechnicon, off Belgrave Square. Eventually the dresses, which were all by Lucile and other eminent dressmakers of the day and so provided an admirable conspectus of high fashion in the last years before 1914, were exhibited with considerable éclat at the Victoria and Albert Museum in 1960. Among the papers there were found not only large quantities of letters from Ronald Firbank to his mother and sister but also some manuscript *juvenilia*, the complete run of notebooks for his novels, and a number of unpublished typescripts, including that of the unfinished novel set in America, and entitled *The New Rythum*. Lieutenant-Colonel Firbank kindly permitted the present selection from the unpublished writings to be made before the whole collection, with a few minor exceptions, was dispersed at Sotheby's on December 12th, 1961. Its full extent can be seen from the Inventory on pages 127–35, which is taken, by the courtesy of Sotheby & Co., from the sale catalogue, itself a notable contribution to Firbank studies, especially in the illustrated version.

Of the correspondence it is enough, here, to remark that it reveals Firbank as a devoted son and brother and the possessor of a fund of practical good sense, in strong contrast to the personality which he habitually presented to the world and projected in his books, though it was not entirely concealed from some of his friends. The notebooks, on the other hand, are of the greatest importance for any study of his methods of work, and some idea of their contents may be gained from the pages reproduced in this book. As these show, they were not common-placebooks but the first stages in the actual composition of a novel, after the general plan, the setting and the characters were in his head. He would then note down innumerable phrases, bits of description, snatches of dialogue and so on — often in numerous alternative versions — of which only about one-tenth, it has been estimated, were ever used. The habit went back at least to his time at Cambridge, when Sir Coleridge Kennard was let into the secret of the carefully kept slips that were the forerunners of the notebooks. From his earliest years Firbank had been precociously observant of the details of social behaviour, and he evidently took immense pains to get the inflexions of the spoken word, however preposterous or inconsequent its content, exactly right. His reward was the astonishing success with which his great fête or party scenes convey the 'feel' of a large social gathering. As he gained experience he was able to reduce the extent of these preparatory labours: *Vainglory* and *Inclinations* had required fifteen and ten notebooks respectively; for *Prancing Nigger* and *The Eccentricities of Cardinal Pirelli* he managed with three and four.

The blank between *Odette* and *The Artificial Princess* now turns out to have been a sort of desultory apprenticeship, which is represented by the typescripts numbered 16 to 24 in the Inventory. The discovery of early unpublished writings often poses a difficult problem of conscience for their author's family and his publishers, especially when the author's own intentions are as clear as Firbank's. At some time in later life he went through these typescripts and marked them all 'Not to be published' (or 'Not to publish') 'RF' except *Impressions d'Automne*, which had already appeared in an obscure

periodical in 1905, and *Lady Appledore's Mésalliance: an
artificial pastoral*, apparently written at Cambridge
(1906–9), on which he wrote '?Revise considerably in
places — if — '. The initials are evidence that the review
took place some time after his change of style from
Arthur (or A. A. R.) Firbank to Ronald Firbank in 1915,
which marked the real start of his public career as
a writer; and since his decisions could hardly have
been reversed on the ground either of merit or (as yet) of
the claims of scholarship, they have been respected. Ac-
cordingly, this book contains *Lady Appledore* in full but
only excerpts from the other unpublished pieces. The
opportunity has also been taken to reprint *A Study in
Temperament* — not quite consistently, perhaps, since
Firbank himself dropped it when *Odette* was re-issued in
1916; but it is of some importance for the understanding
of his early development and, having so far only appeared
in a book which sold less than a hundred copies, is
virtually unknown.

It is now much clearer than it was that even in Firbank's salad days the amused and mocking observer of
social life developed *pari passu* with the aesthete: indeed
it seems from certain very early pieces which reminded
Sotheby's cataloguer of Daisy Ashford, that the former
represented his original bent and that the latter was
a later growth fostered by outside influences. In any
case the newly discovered writings are about equally
divided between these two, sharply contrasted types, each
of which has its exemplar in his first book. On the
aesthetic, the *Odette* side of him (as we may call it for
convenience, though it ranges all the way from the fairy-
tale innocence of Odette herself to the passionate languors
of *True Love*), he was truly Ninety-ish in his preciousness,

his orientation towards France, his typical surrender to the charms of the Catholic Church, as also in some other aspects of his personal life, where his money enabled him to turn luxurious dreams into reality; but the other side of him had quite different affiliations. There was, however, one English writer, often treated as the representative man of the Nineties, who was equally at home in all these styles and whose works could have furnished the model for any one of these pieces; but for the 'aesthetic' ones at least, there were numerous other possible sources of inspiration, and whether it was something of Wilde's or another writer's or simply some friend or mentor that first turned Firbank's attention to the French Decadents, he was soon well versed in them and open to their influence at first hand: in fact Sir Coleridge Kennard has traced *Odette* to a story of Francis Jammes, and *The Mauve Tower* reads almost like a parody of Maeterlinck — interspersed, it is true, with echoes of *Salome*. On his other side, however, the direct influence of Wilde's comedies is plain to see — let anyone who doubts it read the extracts from *A Disciple from the Country* in this book — but in this vein Firbank was never a mere imitator. Though there is much of Wilde, the transformation has already begun, and with Lady Georgia Blueharnis, Mrs Farley (who had only twelve expressions and wanted so much to have another), Mrs Creamway and Mrs Blossome, Firbank's world, to adapt an expression of Kennard's, is beginning to be peopled.

The reception of his books in America, beginning with *Prancing Nigger*, had given him his only taste of anything like success, and it was doubtless to follow it up that in the last year of his life, when he knew his time was short, he embarked on a novel set in New York. 'Since I was

never there,' he wrote from Cairo, where he spent the
winter of 1925, to his American publisher — but perhaps
the qualifying clause might have been omitted — 'you
may be sure it'll be the New Jerusalem before I have done
with it. However, I hope to come out next year and
develop it all.' That hope was never fulfilled, but in the
meantime, as the *Memoir*, after quoting the passage,
relates, he asked for a dictionary of American slang and
colloquialisms, anticipating a 'sore need of a few really
racy words — expressions of the *soil*.' So far as any negro
characters were concerned, he was presumably already
fairly well equipped in this respect, but the two notebooks
for *The New Rythum* show how industriously he used the
only means at his disposal. As for the book itself, it is
difficult to judge even so substantial a fragment fairly, but
one thing is certain: New York or New Jerusalem, this
last vision of the Firbank world, with its pervading atmosphere of a ballroom in Chedorlahomor[1] fanned, in de-
fiance of Nature, by breezes from the isles of Greece, is
the authentic thing. The fantastic inventions — who but
Firbank could have thought of those indoor strawberry
beds? — the 'crush' scenes, the fashionable flagellantes
and their slightly ambiguous clergy, the daring little
jokes and naughty innuendoes — everything definable
that his faithful votaries have a right to expect is there;
and if the magic seems to any of them a shade less potent
than of old, may not the change be in them? Perhaps only
those who have discovered Firbank more or less recently,
for whom *The New Rythum* is just his latest book, instead
of a come-back by a long retired idol of one's youth, can
say whether it is up to standard or not.

Finally, a word about the illustrations. Firbank had

[1] A *faubourg* of Sodom, as readers of *The Flower beneath the Foot* will remember.

HEATHER AND RONALD FIRBANK
a nursery photograph, date unknown

RONALD FIRBANK

photo by Lavender of Bromley, no date

little confidence in the camera as the recorder of his appearance: he preferred the artists, and it is said that the Bertram Park photograph which forms the frontispiece of the *Memoir* is the only one that he would allow to be published. (Incidentally, the inscription 'A. A. R. Firbank 1917' which appears there shows that the original must have been intended for a member of his family, who never recognized his change of style.) Fortunately, however there are several surviving photographs of him (two are reproduced as Plates IV and V) taken at the time he was learning Spanish in Madrid at the age of eighteen or nineteen — this was when 'Lambert Orme' first crossed the path of Harold Nicolson, whose description of him begins: 'It would be impossible, I feel, to actually be as decadent as Lambert Orme looked.' Whether 'decadent' is the adjective that springs most naturally to mind at the sight of these photographs is a matter of individual experience; but Harold Nicolson was far from being on oath in *Some People*, and in any case he was more concerned there with the famous walk and other mannerisms than with looks as they appear in a static representation, though the underlip that 'would come to rest below his upper teeth' is certainly authentic: it is confirmed by a later photograph and a drawing of Augustus John's. An invitation in Nicolson's hand also shows that the episode of the ride, when Lambert Orme surprised him by proving a much better horseman than himself, is at least broadly historical.

The two photographs of his rooms in Trinity Hall, which Mr Vyvyan Holland has described in his contribution to the *Memoir*, are of particular interest because Firbank never set up a home of his own, but after leaving Cambridge lived in an endless succession of hotels and furnished rooms. There were certain objects which, we are told, he took with him wherever he went — one of them, a framed photograph of Lady Firbank in court dress, can be distinguished in Plate IX — but this room is the only example we have of an interior substantially of his own making. Certainly, like Lambert Orme's rooms at Oxford, it is 'not in the least like the rooms of an undergraduate'; indeed, anyone who saw the photograph without a clue to its identity would probably take it to represent the typically crowded drawing-room of an Edwardian lady of means and cultivated, but not very definite, taste.

After the hot room the cold plunge. Mr Holland, who saw Firbank in shorts at Cambridge more than once, could never quite convince himself that they had been put on for use; but there is no room for scepticism about Plate VII: on the original cutting in the family album, the second figure from the right is clearly identified as Ronald Firbank in his own hand. Whether or not the event it depicts helped to preserve him from having his rooms 'ragged', it is a warning against over-confidence in coherence as the test of truth.

That no one could have actually been as Firbankian as Firbank appeared must always have been obvious if one stopped to ask oneself the question; but it needed positive evidence, such as his letters provide, that he had a businesslike side to him, to bring this truth home and add a certain solidity, the third dimension as it were, to his 'image', thereby making him more accessible and human, though many curiosities remain unsatisfied. The many discarded writings, for their part, spring no surprises, call for no new assessment; but they and the notebooks produce a similar effect — the former, by showing that his literary life was rather more consistent than had been supposed, the latter by displaying something of the labour that went to the preparation of the 'mere thistledown' (as he once called it) of his books.

A Study in Temperament

ARTHUR ANNESLEY RONALD FIRBANK

A STUDY IN TEMPERAMENT

LADY AGNES CHARTERS leaned back in a Louis XIV
chair and critically glanced at herself reflected in a tall
mirror. Certainly the delicate green brocade of the *grande
siècle* made a foil for her crown of golden hair which her
women friends charitably attributed to Art. She was
wearing black that day — a long, clinging gown that
coiled about her like a dusky snake; her white hands,
covered in jewels, shone like glow-worms in the twilight.

'There is no one like Lucile for black,' thought she, 'I
am a symphony of black, green, and gold.' Lady Agnes
remained looking at her reflection through half-closed
eyes. 'If only I could persuade Guy to give me those
emeralds, how lovely they would look in my hair!' She
was noted for having the most beautiful hair in London.
It is so nice to be noted for something!

Lady Agnes was always at home Fridays; she hated it,
but then, as she said to her friend, Lord Sevenoaks, she
felt so free when it was all over; so this particular afternoon, Lady Agnes chose a becoming and shady corner in
her boudoir, and waited.

She was expecting a poetess, her sister-in-law, and,
perhaps, her husband. She so seldom saw him, but then
there is something so very early Victorian in seeing one's
husband, except, of course, sometimes at meals.

Lady Agnes yawned.

'How very dull life is,' she said to herself. 'I haven't
seen Sevenoaks for a whole week.'

A bell rang.

'I hope it isn't my sister-in-law,' thought Lady Agnes. She looked at herself in the glass, and ran her hand lightly over her hair.

'I think I shall dye my hair *very* gradually to red,' she said, 'I am so tired of gold; of course those yellow tea roses match beautifully, but I think that yellow is becoming monotonous.' She got up and went to a little table covered with books, and picked up a small volume bound in grey. 'A touch of grey will improve my dress,' she thought as she seated herself in the shady corner again.

Someone was coming upstairs. Lady Agnes opened the book, and found it was one of Maeterlinck's plays.

She hoped it was the poetess. It is so delightful to be seen reading Maeterlinck! So decadent!

But it was only her sister-in-law.

'Mrs and Miss Corba,' said the butler, and disappeared.

'My dearest Agnes!' said Mrs Corba.

'My darling Lettice!' said Lady Agnes.

'I have brought Lobelia,' remarked Mrs Corba, standing aside to show her daughter. 'She is so longing to know Miss — the new poetess.'

'Miss Hester Q. Tail. She is an American.'

'I am always a little nervous of Americans,' said Mrs Corba. 'But Lobelia, of course, having literary tastes — '

'What have you been reading, Aunt Agnes?' asked Lobelia.

'A — A French Author,' said Lady Agnes vaguely. (How trying of Lobelia!)

'I should think,' continued Lobelia, 'that it was very bad for one's eyes reading in the dark.'

(One's relations!)

22

A gaunt figure loomed in the doorway, surmounted by a pair of glistening pince-nez.

'Miss Tail,' announced the butler.

'How sweet of you, Miss Tail, to come! I have a kindred spirit longing to sit at your feet and become a disciple,' said Lady Agnes.

'I am so pleased to meet you, Miss Tail,' smiled Mrs Corba. 'This is my daughter Lobelia, and she would so love your autograph for her collection. We have both read your poems on "The Unseen", and Lobelia can quote long passages . . . about little Minnie finding her mother in Heaven.'

'I shall be most happy in signing myself Sincerely, Hester Q. Tail,' said the poetess, 'and it gives me great pleasure, Miss Corba, to find one so appreciative of my work. In America there have been nineteen editions of "Minnie in Heaven". In England, I am sorry to say, only two.'

Then turning to Mrs Corba:

'But tell me, *dear* Mrs Corba, are you *the* Mrs Corba?'

Mrs Corba looked alarmed.

'I don't know what you can have heard . . .' she began.

'Oh, I hope I have said *nothing*,' said Miss Tail, 'only you know one always reads about your dresses in *The Peacock*.'

Mrs Corba looked relieved.

'Ah!' she said, 'I only wish that all literary people could be exterminated.'

Miss Tail stiffened.

'I should not call the fashion column in *"The Peacock" literature*,' she remarked.

The dispute was ended by the arrival of Lord Sevenoaks.

'How are *you*, Agnes?' he asked.

'Very bored,' she sighed.

'Who isn't?' said Lord Sevenoaks, sitting down beside her.

'Dearest Lettice,' murmured Lady Agnes, 'do show Miss Tail my fans: they are in the yellow drawing-room.'

'I hear you fainted at the Gordons' dance,' Lord Sevenoaks said as soon as they were alone.

Lady Agnes smiled.

'I didn't *really* faint, only . . . well, the room was hot at supper, the table was smothered with red roses, I don't know which looked the redder, the women or the roses! and then . . . well, it is so nice to be different to everyone else, isn't it? So . . . well . . . oh! Guy, I am so *horribly* bored!'

'My dear Agnes, you want an object in life. Art alone isn't enough. Grub Street is so very grimy, and good works are out of date. But aren't there other objects? Isn't there *another* object? If you would only look for it, the search would not be long, and then — '

'You talk in parables,' exclaimed Lady Agnes.

'Well, then, if you would only leave your husband and come away with me, we would go abroad and . . .'

'Don't, Guy; someone will hear you.'

'You are so cautious, Agnes, I don't understand you; you say you love me, and yet — '

'I am not happy with my husband,' said Lady Agnes, 'but then so few women are — at least, in our set.'

'Then you won't come?'

'I cannot, I daren't! Think of the scandal!'

'You should rather say, think of the evening papers!'

'Goose!' laughed Lady Agnes. 'But I shall see you Sunday at the Princess's, shan't I?'

Mrs Corba, who had taken Miss Tail a small personally conducted tour through the five reception rooms, now returned.

'I so love clever people,' she was saying, 'and may I call you Hester?'

'Oh *do*!' said Miss Tail.

Lobelia fixed her eyes upon an Indian idol that stood on the piano, surrounded with iris.

'Agnes is so aesthetic,' ejaculated her sister-in-law.

'I love idols,' said Lord Sevenoaks, joining the conversation.

'Don't talk about idols,' whispered Lady Agnes in a low voice, 'or Miss Tail may try to make an epigram.'

'The ideal idol,' began Miss Tail, and paused.

'Yes?' asked Lobelia anxiously.

'Is made in Japan!' said Miss Tail.

Lobelia looked disappointed; she had hoped for something soulful.

'Do you take cream and sugar, Miss Tail?' asked Lady Agnes.

'A little milk,' said Miss Tail dreamily.

'You are very musical, Miss Corba, I should say?' inquired the poetess, after having mesmerized a plate of bread and butter.

Lobelia looked very pleased.

'Oh no! I am not very musical,' she replied modestly, 'but mama is.'

'I always said I should have liked to marry Paderewski,' said Mrs Corba.

'And you married a captain in the Navy! How inconsistent!'

'Not so inconsistent as you think,' remarked Lobelia. 'Mama always says that papa reminded her of Lohengrin,

25

which is her favourite opera. So Paderewski being un-
available, mama took Lohengrin!'

'And does he remind you of Lohengrin *now*?' asked
Miss Tail.

'No, the idyll only lasted a fortnight. We spent our
honeymoon yachting in the Mediterranean, and . . .'

'Mama is not a good sailor,' interposed Lobelia. . . .

'This is unhappily an age of facts and realities,' said
Miss Tail. 'There is no romance in modern life.'

'I should have loved to have lived in the Bible period,'
said Lobelia, religiously. 'How beautiful to have followed
the Saints!' Lobelia was engaged to a clergyman.

'How very true — ' replied Miss Tail; then, after a
pause, 'modern life is only remarkable for its want of
profile, and lack of manners. To be smart is to be artificial. To be artificial is to be smart. There is not a man or
woman in London society that dares to be him or herself.
We are surrounded by invisible laws and conventions,
we all sin, and cover our sins in chiffon and diamonds.
The chiffon is quite transparent, everyone can see through
it, still chiffon is a veil, and then the diamonds! We are
all vulgar at heart, and if the diamonds glitter, what does
it matter where they come from or how they are bought?
To be artificial, and to be a little more improbable and
impossible than one's neighbour, is to be a perfect success!'

Lady Agnes looked shocked. She had not been looking
at Miss Tail, but at her own reflection in a mirror.

This was of course the result of knowing such people!
She regretted ever having asked Miss Tail; if she continued receiving her she would soon have a reputation of
harbouring socialists, perhaps Nihilists — how dreadful!

Lobelia looked interested; as a future clergyman's wife

she felt she ought to uphold Miss Tail. Still she didn't like the remark about profiles. Lobelia had no profile; she knew it, and did her best not to show hers. But it is almost impossible to go through life without showing one's profile — at dinner-parties, for instance.

Agnes trailed over to Lord Sevenoaks. 'I want to show you,' she said, 'a new picture that my husband has bought; it is in the white drawing-room.'

Lord Sevenoaks followed her.

'Who are the two ladies with Miss Tail?' he asked as soon as they were out of hearing.

'My sister-in-law and her daughter,' replied Lady Agnes.

'*Which* is the mother?' asked Lord Sevenoaks.

'The younger-looking of the two. Lobelia, her daughter, always wears such morbid-looking hats, they make her look quite ten years older than she really is. Her mother always wears black — now she is losing her figure. She always pretends to be in mourning for someone, simply as an excuse for wearing black; she has been in black now for three seasons.'

'In other words,' said Lord Sevenoaks, 'she has been losing her figure for three years.'

Lady Agnes regretted now having left her guests. Guy was so impulsive. She felt a little afraid. She chattered on and on, and at last ceased.

'Where is the picture?' asked Lord Sevenoaks.

Lady Agnes laughed a little nervously.

'This is it,' she said.

It was a mystical Madonna. A woman, with a long pale face, leaning out of the clouds, the sins and sorrows of the whole world gathered in the wearied eyelids and the red-gold of her hair. They were both silent. The last grey light of the London twilight fell on the picture, and the long pale face of the Madonna seemed drawn in pain.

'How beautiful her eyes are, they are full of pity,' said Lord Sevenoaks. 'She is alive, see how her lips are parted, one can almost hear her breathe!'

'Don't look at her any more or I shall be jealous,' cried Lady Agnes.

'Don't, Agnes!' said Lord Sevenoaks. 'It hurts me to hear you talk like that.'

Lady Agnes laughed a little bitterly.

'I hate sentiment,' she said.

The room grew darker and darker, and the Madonna's face looked like a ghost from the white brocaded wall. The room smelt vaguely of lilies.

Lord Sevenoaks looked from the painted face of the Madonna to the painted face of Lady Agnes.

'Come,' exclaimed Lady Agnes a little brusquely, 'we are getting morbid. Let us go back to the others.'

'Not yet!' said Lord Sevenoaks.

'Not yet?' asked Lady Agnes.

'No, Agnes, listen to me. You are not happy here, you have told me so — then let us be brave — and — and defy the evening papers! Let us go away, there will be a scandal at first, but what of that? There will soon be another to take its place.'

Lady Agnes laughed nervously.

'I will tell you Sunday,' she said, and went quickly back to her guests in the yellow drawing-room.

* * * * *

Lord Sevenoaks remained behind a few minutes after Lady Agnes had left. How strange women are, thought he. 'I believe if Agnes leaves her husband—but oh! she doesn't seem able to *feel*, she has read so much that she has lost *herself*, she has become cold, artificial, and almost cruel, yet with such a husband as hers!' Lord Sevenoaks started.

'Come, old man,' he said to himself, 'you are becoming sentimental.' And yet, thought he, I remember Agnes when quite a wee mite! And he sat staring into the fire dreaming. The Madonna looked down on him from the walls, and her eyes seemed to dim with tears!

*　　*　　*　　*　　*

That night as her maid brushed her hair, Lady Agnes's thoughts seemed troubled.

'Shall I bolt?' she asked herself.

She looked critically at herself in a long mirror.

Then she said to her maid: 'I may go down to Brighton next Sunday. I want you to have my things ready in case I go.'

She looked at herself in the glass again and began dreaming.

'I am very beautiful,' she thought, 'but I think it would be an improvement to dye my hair red — very gradually, of course — I should so hate anyone to notice — '

Her maid closed the door quietly, and left her for the night.

The half-hour struck — the three-quarters — Lady Agnes rose.

'Yes, I shall certainly dye my hair red,' she said.

Lady Appledore's Mésalliance

AN ARTIFICIAL PASTORAL

by

A. A. R. FIRBANK

LADY APPLEDORE'S MÉSALLIANCE

ALTHOUGH the Venetian blinds were down in the white-panelled room where Wildred sat, it was impossible to shut the sunlight entirely out.

It came in hesitatingly through the thick silk draperies, and, pale as a moonbeam, slid over the Persian carpet, warily like a cat.

He did not notice it for some time, he was too much engrossed in his own sorrow, but presently he felt the sun's warm touch creep through his body, and with a weary sigh he lifted up his head.

'Hullo!' he exclaimed, as he noticed the sun shining upon his hands. 'What are you doing here? Didn't they tell you that I was not at home today? What are the use of Venetian blinds, I should like to know?' and going over to the long windows, he pulled the lazily dropping blinds up with a rush.

'After all, what's the use of sitting in the dark?' he murmured.

The brilliant afternoon had brought out streams of carriages, that wound slowly down Piccadilly towards the Park. From behind the hood of each carriage fluttered parasols, like delicate full-blown flowers, and beyond the high green railings, on the opposite side of the way, the trees in St James's Park had begun to join their shadows in faint patterns upon the grass.

'At this hour tomorrow,' thought Wildred, 'I shall have started my new life. Oh! what will it feel like, I wonder, watering Orchids, and making wreaths of Stephanotis for Lord Appledore's grave? However, I would sooner do that,' he murmured, 'than stay in town, and go into some sordid city office, and bear the humiliation of being gradually dropped by my former friends.'

He looked round the dainty white and gold room, and there were tears in his eyes.

Life seemed so hard just then!

On a grand piano stood an open piece of music by Debussy, and in long vases, everywhere scattered about the room, breathed drooping pink Tea-roses, amidst profusions of Wisteria.

A large packing-case stood in the centre of the room; how unsympathetic, how out of keeping it looked!

'Still I must make a beginning,' he told himself, and stooping down he began to fill the box with favourite books and music.

'I don't suppose that there will be a piano there,' he said. 'How should there be? And I must just take my simplest clothes, these silk pyjamas are far too smart, but then I can't afford to buy woollen ones, so here goes!' and he rolled them up round a family photograph of a lady in Court dress.

'Poor Aunt Cynthia! she is about the only one of them who would sympathize with my experiment, and even she might be a little horrified!' and with a sigh of regret he gently laid a large paper copy of Maeterlinck's *Ariane et Barbe-Bleue* into the ugly wooden case.

When the packing was finished, he dressed himself carefully and went round to Half Moon Street to fetch his cousin, Sir George Liss.

He had already engaged a table for dinner at the Ritz.

'After all why shouldn't I spend my last evening as I

like, and as George pays for the Opera box, it would be really mean if I took him to dine with me at Lockhart's, and it's all through him, too, that I got the place.'

*   *   *   *   *

'I have a letter from Lady Appledore about you,' Sir George Liss said to him at dinner.

'She is in terrible trouble about a mauve and black Orchid that she fears is going to die, and her Maréchal Niel Roses, she says, were not nearly so fine last year as the year before.'

'Her mauve and black Orchids shall be my special care,' murmured Wildred as he sipped his champagne. 'I remember seeing her with them once at a Court ball, she had a long chain of them falling from her shoulder in a shower over her train, and her husband was trying to act as a paling, to prevent them from being crushed.'

'Yes, do be gentle with the Orchids, and try to make the Roses big again,' his cousin begged him; 'remember if anything goes wrong, it is I that will be blamed for having recommended you.'

They arrived at Covent Garden just as Isolde was swallowing the Love-potion, and all through the stormy music that followed, Wildred sat with closed eyes allowing the music to pierce through him.

How frightful his situation really was! Apparently he was practically penniless; until everything was settled, which might take another six months, he had no income at all. To have had everything, to lose everything. . . .

He leaned his long pale face upon his hand.

How beautiful the music was, and this was probably the last time he would ever come here. How hard it was to give up all that made life worth living. . . .

He turned as his cousin touched his arm.

'Look!' Sir George said, 'do you see the woman with the aigrette in the box opposite?'

'You mean the woman fanning herself?'

'Yes. That is Lady Appledore.'

'How very amusing!' said Wildred, peering at her through his opera glasses.

* * * * *

Nobody else got out at Minster-le-Hope.

It was one of those ideal-looking little villages, that one sometimes passes through in the train, but where one never stops at. The Foxgloves grew right down on to the line, amidst high bracken and ferns, and all around stretched a magnificent oak forest. The name 'Minster-le-Hope' was written in dissipated-looking scarlet geraniums, that were doing their best to escape into a bed of violet-coloured Poppies.

With a sense of relief, Wildred got down from the hot third class carriage.

How exquisite it was to breathe the pure evening air!

The white vapour from the engine rose falteringly into the paling sky; on all sides glimmered the wild Broom, and the Gorse.

'How iniquitous it is!'

There was no conveyance of any kind at the station.

'We have so few visitors at Minster-le-Hope,' the station master explained, 'and then they only come to visit the church. Oliver Cromwell's mother is buried there, and there's also a niece of a Cabinet Minister, who died only the other day.'

'I have not come sight-seeing,' Wildred said, 'but want

to get to Wiston, Lady Appledore's place, which is, I believe, about three miles away.'

'Are you the new gardener?' the station master inquired.

Wildred stared. 'Yes, but how should you know?'

The station master laughed. 'All Minster-le-Hope knewed you was coming,' he explained.

'Then do tell me where I can get a carriage,' asked Wildred.

'A carriage! Young man, there is no such thing, but if she is not using it, you may borrow Mrs Maley's cart from the "Horse & Crown".'

'How very tiresome,' thought Wildred, and leaving his box at the station, he set out on foot for the village.

It was not very far. He could see the Norman tower of the Church through the dark foliage of the trees. A little beyond shone lights from cottage windows.

He had no difficulty in finding the place, and whilst the cart was being got ready, he seated himself on a wooden bench outside the inn, and watched the bats rush past, and the distant hills grow fainter and fainter in the failing light.

The moon had risen when at last they started.

A signpost, looking like a very thin Pierrot, pointed a white arm towards Wiston.

Wildred was too much occupied with his own thoughts to notice the country through which they passed. He recollected a certain evening in Berlin, at a dinner at the English Embassy, he had told a diplomat's wife that should he ever be obliged to earn his living he would become a gardener. And she had laughed, and thought the idea charming. 'Delicious,' she had said, 'to pass one's life arranging nothing more dangerous than flowers!

Think of the joy of choosing a colour scheme for an herbaceous border! and the beneficial result of a quiet mind to the complexion, which is so difficult to acquire in Berlin!'

How little he had thought then that one day his idle words would come true! And now that they had, his mind misgave him dreadfully . . . and besides, he had to admit it, he felt absurdly nervous of meeting Bartholomew, the head gardener. Whatever would he be like? and what should they talk about? 'I hope I shan't see very much of him,' he murmured, 'and I wonder, if he is married, whether I ought to leave cards on his wife?'

The cart jolted through a plantation of young larch trees, that hung their drooping branches so low over the road that their soft green twigs, wet with dew, swept their faces, on, out on to a misty common where a windmill slowly turned, and turned, like a revolving crucifix.

Suddenly they stopped before a long red brick wall.

'Is there anything wrong with the horse?' Wildred inquired.

'The horse is healthy enough!' the driver answered. 'These are the gardens.'

Wildred sprang down, glad that the drive had come to an end. The driver rang a rusty-looking bell.

Over the garden wall, that seemed very old, Wildred could see the tops of fruit trees, through which the stars were shining. The wall ran along the highroad for nearly a quarter of a mile, and seemed to end in a clock tower, that was probably the stables.

The sound of a key, turning in the little green door in the wall, made him look round.

A pretty, but untidily coiffed girl peeped cautiously out.

'What do you want?' she asked, 'if it's father he's on duty and cannot come.'

'I'm the new gardener,' answered Wildred.

'Oh indeed, then come in.'

She opened the door wide, and stood aside to let him pass.

'Carry the box across to the room above the potting-shed,' she told the driver, and turning to Wildred: 'Come now, and have supper, for you must need it,' she said.

He followed her down a dark shrubbery. There were wild flowers growing everywhere under the trees; he noticed a few late Hyacinths, and numberless Foxgloves.

'Have you come far?' she asked, turning and looking at him curiously.

'From London,' he answered.

'Ah! I was only there once . . . to see the Queen's Jubilee. I lost my silver brooch there,' she added as though talking to herself.

They turned an abrupt corner, which brought them in sight of the gardener's cottage. It was covered in creeper and Clematis, and looked rather damp, Wildred thought.

'Come in,' she said, and led the way down an unlit passage.

In the kitchen his supper was waiting for him — some soup and an Irish stew. He sat down to please her, although he had no appetite.

There was a canary on the table, in a very small cage, that now and again sang a few notes to show that it was still awake. His hostess took some knitting, and drawing her chair up beside his began to talk.

'The family are still away,' she said, 'but Lady Appledore comes back tomorrow. Miss Iris is in the North with Fraülein, she has had measles, and has gone to Bury St Edmunds to get well. You will be required to arrange the jardinières with plants tomorrow morning. Have you ever arranged before? Lady Appledore likes always blue or white flowers for her boudoir, and sometimes it's rather difficult. I don't know why there are so few blue flowers. She is a very eccentric lady, they say, and hard to please.'

The girl paused a moment to count the stitches in the sock she was making.

'Sometimes,' she went on, 'there are parties, and I get a glimpse of the swell folk through the trees. My! you should see the clothes they wear of an evening. I wonder they don't all catch cold. Miss Grantham, Lady Appledore's maid, once gave me, in return for a spray of Passion flowers, a little box of her ladyship's complexion. I have got it still, hidden away in an old boot, lest father should find it. He does not hold with them painted courtesans, he says, and their ways are not ours.'

She paused for breath, and getting up, flung a cloth over the canary's cage, as the bird had commenced to sing.

'It is all very interesting what you tell me,' Wildred said, as he finished his supper. 'And now, please, where can I find your father?'

'Father is not to be disturbed,' she said, beginning to clear away the table, 'he is sitting up all night with a sick Orchid.'

*   *   *   *   *

It must have been five o'clock the next morning when Wildred awoke. The sun was shining straight into his eyes, through the open window. From his bed he could see the tops of the fruit trees, clouded in pink blossom, already on the verge of falling.

'I am so glad it is fine,' he murmured, 'I couldn't have borne it to be wet my first morning, and the birds! Oh, listen!'

He sprang up and ran to the window. The room looked over an orchard bounded by mellow red brick walls, upon which Peach and Cherry trees were spread under voluminous looking nets.

'The effect of the trailing white clouds, over the cherry blossom, and the long blue-green grass, is worthy of Daubigny,' he told himself, as he proceeded to dress.

His toilet ended, he wondered what he should do.

'I suppose I had better go and look for Bartholomew, and introduce myself,' and putting on a straw hat he went down into the garden.

'I shall probably find him in a greenhouse,' Wildred thought, and sure enough in the first greenhouse he peeped into, he found an old man sleeping, his head carefully enveloped in a long grey shawl.

'It must be he,' Wildred told himself, and clearing his throat to attract attention: 'Good morning,' he said.

The old man opened one eye, and stared at Wildred.

'Are you Sam's successor?' he inquired.

'I expect I am, at all events, I am the new gardener. I am sorry,' he added, 'to hear that you have an Orchid that is dying, I hope it will recover.'

Old Bartholomew took the shawl from his head.

'The mauve Orchid is a little better this morning,' he answered, 'but she is low, very low. She passed as quiet a night as I could expect, and has closed her leaves now, thank God, and sleeps peaceful as a child. Speak softly, for she must not be disturbed. About one o'clock,' he

continued in a whisper, 'I thought that she had gone . . .
I lit my lanthorn and had a look at her. She had turned
all black. Only a tinge of mauve round the heart told me
that she still breathed.'

'How perfectly terrible,' murmured Wildred sympathetically. 'But on such a lovely summer's morning, I
am sure it cannot die; the song of the birds will give it
dreams of the Jungle from whence it came. Think! poor
flower, how it must pine for the wild nature that gave it
birth. Perhaps on those endless afternoons when the sun
scorched the Palm trees, and all the Jungle seemed shat-
tered with heat, some green and silver snake may have
coiled itself languorously around it, and played with its
black and purple leaves! And on the white starry nights,
when the Birds of Paradise, in the tall Gum trees, cast
their long shower plumes across the moon, and the forest
smelt sweet of Arum lilies . . . Ah!' he broke off, 'think
of the difference of its present surroundings. A red pot
on a shelf at Wiston!'

'And now will you kindly take this broom and sweep
the lawn before the house,' old Bartholomew asked him,
'for her ladyship will be here today, and she does not like
to see a fallen leaf.'

Wildred left old Bartholomew to his meditations,
wondering what Lady Appledore could be like, if she
disliked to step on a fallen leaf.

'It probably reminds her that she is growing old,' he
told himself, as he began to sweep.

But there was really no sign of a leaf anywhere, and it
seemed to him cruel to behead the Daisies.

It was the month of June, and the air was full of the
fragrance of new-born flowers. Across the park the sun
poured down its gold on to the eager Buttercups, and

encouraged the drooping Cowslips. The birds were everywhere; they flew down from the shadow of the trees, and opened their grey wings to the warm morning, singing. Through the branches of a tall Lime, the stable clock pointed to half past six.

'It is frightfully early,' Wildred told himself, 'and I think I shall lie down under this tree for a while, and smoke a cigarette.'

He stretched himself out on the grass, in the shadow of a Lime, and watched the mist gathering in the Park over the woods. Overhead a wood-pigeon cooed deliciously, she seemed to be brooding over some great happiness . . . so soft was her voice. The long Elizabethan house was just visible to him from where he lay. Every blind drawn down, it slept solemnly on, heedless of the bright morning.

At seven o'clock Wildred saw the glass door, leading on to the terrace, open, and a housemaid appeared, broom in hand.

'I suppose I had better go and find out what flowers are wanted,' he murmured, and crossed the lawn to the open door.

'Good morning,' he said to the housemaid, who was standing on the doorstep, apparently dusting a Rose, 'can you tell me where I shall find the butler?'

'Mr Perfect is still in bed,' replied the housemaid; 'when the family are away, he rarely descends before eleven o'clock. You are the new gardener, I suppose?'

'I am,' Wildred answered, 'and I should be much obliged to you if you would show me what flowerpots I must fill.'

'I shall be charmed,' she murmured. 'What is your name? Mine is Annie.'

'And mine Wildred,' he informed her. 'I am sorry I have not a card with me.'

'Oh do not trouble, besides it is not etiquette for an underservant to keep visiting cards. This is the drawing-room. I will leave you to look round, I shall be back in a moment,' and she darted away.

'What wonderful Dresden!' Wildred exclaimed, looking about him, 'and this, I suppose must be the famous Flemish tapestry, and these the rock crystal wall lights that disappeared from the Vatican! Really Lady Appledore has the most perfect drawing-room.'

He wandered through the room admiring everything, now and again peeping at the title-page of a book, or stooping down to look at a photograph.

He recognized, with a start, a portrait of his aunt, the Duchess of St Andrews, standing on the grand piano, with her autograph 'Queenie' written in hieroglyphics across her train, and on the same instrument his cousin, the beautiful Miss Clodah Forrester, the society actress, was seen in one of her most childlike parts.

'But what difference Mama does it make if I *do* marry Jim?' and her mother's reply, 'But none, dear, none,' Clodah had inscribed in copybook handwriting across the photo, and then in a corner, 'Rôle of Ethel in *The Outcast.*'

'What a shock!' murmured Wildred, pressing his hand to his heart. 'But Clodah, thank God, is in Hungary for the present, and the Duchess rarely comes further south than Newcastle, which she persists in always calling the Frontier. I remember the time she came down from Scotland, to stay with us in Park Street. After waiting dinner for her nearly two hours (mother in the meanwhile having retired for the night with *The Little Flowers of St Francis* and a cornflour pudding), the dreadful peal we suddenly heard from the front door bell. "I hope it's not to say that the Prime Minister has had another relapse," father said, and just then the door flew open, and the Duchess burst in, and flung herself into poor mother's dressing-room saying that she was without a nightgown or a maid, as she had lost them both crossing the Frontier. How long ago it all seems!' he said, looking at himself in a Queen Anne mirror, and rather admiring the dead-gold colour of his hair.

At that moment Annie returned. 'If you would please to come this way,' she said, 'I will show you her ladyship's boudoir.'

He followed her up a flight of stairs, into a charming room with bay windows, overlooking the park. The walls were hung mostly in old Dutch needle-work, but here and there from a piece of mahogany panelling hung a rare print.

Alice, the third housemaid, was down on her knees polishing the parquet floor, but she stood up as they entered, and came forward to be introduced.

'This room has never been photographed for the papers like the rest of the house,' she said by way of conversation, 'it is her ladyship's little holy-of-holies. Please be careful when you are putting pots in the Chinese jardinières not to chip them, for they are museum pieces.'

On the staircase Annie pointed out a faded blue and gold box, studded with nails.

'It is always filled with small Almond trees,' she said, 'her ladyship likes it done with nothing else. It was once part of the marriage equipment of Miss Isabella d'Este, a young lady of the Italian Renaissance.'

'Her husband was a Podeſta,' called out Alice over the landing, 'which, Mr Perfeɛt says, means the same thing as a Doge.'

*   *   *   *   *

As he was carrying a basket of peaches and white roses towards the house, for the dinner table, he came suddenly across Lady Appledore.

She had evidently only juſt arrived, for she wore a long grey duſt cloak, and a large black hat, bedecked with oſtrich feathers, that looked very much like London. She was seated in a basket chair, talking to her dogs. A foreign-looking little woman, in a tailor-made gown, ſtood beside her, fanning herself with a magnolia leaf.

'Probably Mademoiselle Doucet, the companion,' thought Wildred, who had heard of her from the gardener's daughter.

He touched his cap to Lady Appledore as he passed, and murmured 'good evening', but she did not seem to notice him, for she went on playing with her dogs.

As he returned with the empty basket, however, she glanced up and called him.

'How is the Orchid?' she inquired.

'Better, I believe, your ladyship, but I have not yet seen it,' Wildred answered.

'You are Wildred, the new gardener, are you not? and you have been three years with Sir George Liss? When you were at Holton, did you have much experience in arranging herbaceous borders? and do you, I wonder, grasp the meaning of colour, which in a gardener, I maintain, is almoſt as important as keeping early hours, and not being tempted into the public house?'

46

'I used to have the reputation of always wearing the most harmonious ties, your ladyship,' he answered humbly.

She raised her eyebrows. 'Really. I am not interested. But do you realize that Paeonies and Lobelia are not suitable together? that flowers can make the most undesirable marriages, just as — ' she raised her large dark eyes to his, and studied his face for the first time.

His curly dim-gold hair, the delicate skin, the beautifully shaped mouth and hands, and his wide grey eyes made her forget what she was saying.

'Have I never seen you before?' she asked, 'but I suppose I must have noticed you at Holton, when I was staying last Easter with Sir George.'

The dressing-gong sounded from the house just then, and she rose to go.

Wildred looked at her in amazement. 'She is perfectly lovely,' he told himself, 'I have never seen anybody quite so beautiful.'

'I shall want you to bring me a large basket of flowers in the morning,' she said, 'choice ones, as they are for decorating the summer house of Apollo.'

'Certainly,' he replied, 'and I think the idea is delightful. Good night, your ladyship.'

She looked at him in astonishment.

'Good night, Wildred,' she said, and went into the house.

He stood for a moment looking after her, tingling with delight. She had called him Wildred!

The bats flew past him, circling wildly, almost brushing him with their wings; from every window lamps showed, shrouded by soft-coloured shades. Oh! if he were in Italy, now he would seize a guitar and sing.

'You fool,' he told himself, 'gardeners are always called by their Christian names.' But how wonderfully she had said it. Wildred. Wildred!

He wandered away from the house, and went towards the park. The long grass was drenched with dew; away beyond the woods the sun was almost out of sight, only on the topmost boughs of the tall Elm trees lingered a ray of gold. He wandered on, attracted in the distance by the gleam of water.

That Greek-looking temple through the trees must be Apollo's summer house.

He drew near.

Emerging from between the delicate marble columns of the temple, as though about to plunge himself into the lake, stood a slim Apollo, his head bent a little forward, peering down at his own white form in the trembling water.

'He looks ever so much more like Narcissus than Apollo,' said Wildred, and seating himself on the river bank he recited to the first moonbeam that touched the lake, a poem of Verlaine.

*　　*　　*　　*　　*

The next morning, the paper said, was the hottest day of the year.

'And to think that I must water the herbaceous borders,' he said; 'how much pleasanter it would be to sit in the orchard with a book!'

He was dressed in an old cricket blazer, and a soft silk shirt open at the neck, his Panama hat well turned down over the eyes.

'It is really delicious to be able to wear what one likes,' he murmured, 'supposing I were in London now, I should be wearing stays and a frock coat. Ugh! How ripe and fresh those peaches look,' he went on admiringly, 'I simply cannot resist them. That ripe, pink-looking peach is, I am sure, the mother of all those little green ones, it would be cruel to take *her*. But these!!' He filled both pockets of his blazer with fruit, and then scrambled up into a beech tree to enjoy it.

The sunlight shining through the leaves was so beautiful that it seemed to him that each leaf must be an emerald, and the song of a thrush, just on a bough above, lulled him to entrancing drowsiness.

In all probability he must have fallen asleep, for presently he became conscious that someone was calling him as though from a great distance. He opened his eyes. 'Yes, what is it?' he murmured.

On the path below stood Lady Appledore, looking up at him in amazement.

'What are you doing up there?' she inquired.

'I felt a little languid,' he explained, 'the morning is so hot.'

'Languid! *Languid!* I never heard of such a thing, I cannot possibly allow you to feel languid whilst my roses perish for water.'

He clambered from his branch, sending down a shower of peach stones, that fell at Lady Appledore's feet.

'You are fond of peaches, I see,' she remarked. 'Do you think that a languid gardener, who makes siestas in trees, and is fond of peaches, is quite the person I want?'

'I am indeed sorry, your ladyship,' Wildred murmured, and he looked so handsome in his garden get-up that Lady Appledore said nothing more.

'I hadn't the heart to send him away,' she told

Mademoiselle Doucet at lunch, 'he has the most beautiful face I have ever seen.'

*   *   *   *   *

That night it rained. How close! how intimate it sounded, pattering down on the thirsty leaves outside!

His room was so full of shadows that he could not see the time. He could just distinguish the dark outline of the trees in the orchard below his window; he had thought that in the country there was always a moon!

'I am afraid all this damp will give the nightingales sore throats,' he told himself, 'and how tiresome that I should have wasted my day in watering Roses when nature herself was only waiting for the opportunity. There is one comfort, I shall have an idle day tomorrow,' and he meditated what books he should read. 'Ronsard in the morning would be charming, and D'Annunzio in the afternoon,' he decided as he fell asleep.

He dreamt of peach stones, and a lady with a lace parasol, whose face he could not see.

He awoke with a start, hearing the sound of gravel thrown against his window-pane.

Old Bartholomew was standing below in the wet.

'Are you dreaming that you was your own master, and would you like your breakfast sent up to you on a tray?' he inquired. 'You may not be aware that it has gone eight.'

'Bother the old man!' exclaimed Wildred, as he dressed. 'I thought I was to have had a quiet morning to myself, and just look at the rain!'

He was told by old Bartholomew when he went downstairs, that it was the day appointed for changing the plants in the house.

Really it was a nuisance to have to trundle palm trees through the wet, but there was no help for it so it seemed.

He found Mademoiselle Doucet in the morning room, having breakfast, when he entered.

'Good morning,' she remarked, 'what an unpleasant day!'

'It is indeed, Mademoiselle, but it will cool the air.'

She continued her breakfast, glancing now and then at a letter by her side.

'Ah, non pas comme ça!' she exclaimed suddenly looking up.

He was endeavouring to squeeze a red Camellia tree into the same jardinière as some Maiden Hair ferns, that seemed most unwilling to yield the desired inch.

'Pas comme ça?' he asked, 'mais alors que voulez vous que je fasse?'

She looked at him in amazement.

'You speak French?' she demanded.

'Yes, Mademoiselle, only a little.'

'Comment donc! but it is extraordinary.'

'How extraordinary?'

'Mais, je ne sais pas, but as a rule, gardeners . . .'

'But, Mademoiselle, I have not *always* been a gardener.'

'No?'

How frightfully imprudent of him, he must take care.

'No,' he remarked smilingly, 'I was once over in Paris — in business there, I was a . . . a . . . an assistant in a hairdresser's shop! Chez Rubens, you know, in the Rue de la Paix.'

'Mon Dieu!' gasped Mademoiselle Doucet, 'then perhaps sometimes you could arrange my hair for me, it is so very troublesome. Ah! what happiness to find a coiffeur from chez Rubens dans un lieu si sauvage, and how delighted Lady Appledore will be!'

*　　*　　*　　*　　*

'My dear, he is no such thing,' Lady Appledore told her, 'and even if he were, I should never dream of allowing him to do my hair.'

They were driving into Minster-le-Hope to meet a nest of plover's eggs that were coming down from town by rail.

'How much less fussy it is to meet a plover's nest than a friend,' Lady Appledore reflected.

'Good afternoon,' she called to the Vicar, who flew past on his bicycle as though he were trying to circumvent the Devil.

'What a glorious day, dear lady,' he called out to her, 'I am hastening to the station to meet my wife.'

'Malheureux!' Mademoiselle Doucet murmured sympathetically, 'but do let us stop at the Post Office and get the letters,' she suggested, 'it's my poor mother's day for writing.'

'She writes very often to you,' Lady Appledore remarked dryly. 'Does she still live at Versailles?'

'Yes, in the Cour la Reine, but oh do look at that field of Buttercups, did you ever see anything quite so golden, on dirait un morceau de . . . de . . .'

'Yes! here's the post,' exclaimed Lady Appledore.

'Are there any letters?' she inquired.

The woman handed them to her. 'Will you take the servants' letters also?' she asked.

'Yes, we may as well, and it will save your son a walk.'

The postmistress beamed on Lady Appledore.

'Such a hot day! What dusty roads! and how unfortunate that Minster-le-Hope wasn't nearer the sea!' She ran

from subject to subject without pausing to breathe. 'Come
and look at my Phloxes,' she invited, 'they are the finest
in all the village. Most of the neighbours only find time
for growing Candytuft, but I thinks no country garden
should be without a bit of Sweet William, and a Colom-
bine or two.'

As they passed down the village street, a face flew to
every window, to see the beautiful lady and the prancing
horses, but Lady Appledore was feeling decidedly bored.
There were no letters of any interest, and the gaping
children, rolling in the dust, failed just then to appeal to
her instinct of the picturesque.

'But who are all the letters for?' inquired Mademoiselle
Doucet with curiosity.

Lady Appledore sorted them out. 'One for Mrs Gwatkin, and all the rest, yes! every one of them! are for the
new gardener.'

'Would it be very wrong, I wonder, to open one,
and see who it was from,' murmured Mademoiselle
Doucet.

'My dear!' exclaimed Lady Appledore horrified, 'how
could you think of such a thing! This one,' she went on,
holding a long lilac-tinted envelope up to the sun, 'is
from the Duchess of St Andrews, I know the handwriting. But why will she always write on such thick
paper? It has been forwarded on from the Pall Mall Club.
Surely, *surely*, the man cannot be a member of the Pall
Mall Club?'

Mademoiselle Doucet shivered. 'I have a presentiment
that he may be a burglar, or an Anarchist,' she said. 'Oh!
dear Lady Appledore, I shall never dare go to sleep tonight, and the key in my bedroom door won't turn.'

'I will have the lock arranged immediately,' Lady

Appledore assured her, 'but do not be nervous, dear Mademoiselle Doucet, for I feel convinced that the only thing that may be destroyed through this man's presence are my flowers.'

'We are in God's hands,' Mademoiselle Doucet said piously, as the carriage turned into the drive, 'and oh look!' she suddenly screamed, shielding herself behind her parasol, 'he is standing there hiding behind a tree, I believe he is taking aim at me with a pistol, and means to fire.'

'Don't be so absurd,' Lady Appledore said, 'and do try and control your mind.'

'Wildred,' she called to him, 'here are letters for you, come and take them.'

He came forward, trying to hide a book behind his back.

Mademoiselle Doucet nearly fainted. 'I see the gleam of the trigger,' she murmured, and closing her eyes waited for the explosion.

'Thank you, your ladyship,' Wildred answered, taking the letters with a slight bow.

'What are you holding behind your back so carefully?' Lady Appledore asked him.

'This,' said Wildred, looking horribly guilty, and holding up a beautifully bound volume.

'May I see?'

He handed it to her.

She looked at him puzzled. 'You read Omar Khayyám, and what a lovely edition! I am afraid you are very extravagant, but better spend your money so than in the public house.'

'And now home,' she said to the coachman.

*　　*　　*　　*　　*

The next day was Sunday.

Dressed all in white, with a large shady hat, garlanded with blue Hortensias, Lady Appledore sat under a lime tree reading.

Her book was a study on the Architecture of Valladolid Cathedral. Lady Appledore loved remote books, the more distant the subject to her everyday life, the more she was charmed.

Novels about Society bored her, although she was fond of reading plays, but a treatise on industries that would have no interest to her in real life, delighted her in books.

Thus, a short essay on the Manufacture of Strawberry-punnets thrilled her to enthusiasm. 'It soothed me, it lulled me like nothing else,' she had told a royal lady, who was complaining of feeling nervous at night.

'It is delicious to know something about the Moors,' she murmured, 'they *must* have been dears.'

The quiet thread of her thoughts was rudely broken upon by Grantham, her maid, who appeared just then with a parasol and a prayer-book.

'Your ladyship will be late for Church,' she remarked, 'it is eleven o'clock already.'

Wildred too had gone into Minster-le-Hope for the morning service.

It was such a delightful old Church, with quaint carved monuments fixed into niches in the wall, and from where Wildred sat he could see the quiet church-yard bathed in full sunshine, and he noticed the simple tomb of Oliver Cromwell's mother, over which a rambling red rose tree cast its flowers.

He sang so well that several people turned to see who was the owner of the warm rich voice, and after the service the Vicar called him aside and asked him to join the choir.

Some of the servants from Wiston were waiting outside in the porch.

'You will have to come and sing to us one evening,' Mr Perfect the butler graciously invited him. 'Arthur, the second footman, plays the banjo, and Violet, the kitchen-maid, is a skilful amateur of the concertina, and when her ladyship is out driving, and all the doors are closed, Squire, the pantry boy, plays us selections on the bassoon.'

Annie and Alice asked him if he were fond of musical comedy, but Mrs Gwatkin, the cook, who had just gone over to the Plymouth Brethren, did not think the subject quite fitted to Sunday, and changed the conversation by alluding to the heat.

'How unpleasant to be a cow!' she said, pointing with her parasol towards the park. 'Poor things! I wonder they don't get sunstroke with no hats on their heads but their horns.'

Mr Perfect agreed. 'But I am no friend to cows,' he said, 'they are such licentious animals. Things as has no tables of kindred and affinity are not to be respected.'

'I wish,' said Lady Appledore to Mademoiselle Doucet, as they passed the servants, 'that Perfect would not wear poor Appledore's clothes, although I know he gave them to him; they do *so* get on my nerves.'

*   *   *   *   *

But it is always the unexpected that happens, and one morning as Wildred was busy digging up cabbages, he was startled to hear a familiar voice behind him.

'My dear Wildred, what on earth are you doing? I had

Signed ARTHUR FIRBANK, 1905

RONALD FIRBANK
photographed by Kaulak, Madrid, 1905

RONALD FIRBANK
photographed by Kaulak, Madrid, 1905

NOBODY KNEW quite WHO SHE
WAS, NOBODY HAD ANYTHING
EXACTLY AGAINST HER.
ONE SAW HER EVERYWHERE,
AND SHE WAS ALWAYS SO
BEAUTIFULLY
DRESSED. SHE
SAID HER HUSBAND
WAS "IN BUSINESS"
AND EVERYONE
ADMIRED HER
FOR SO CLEVERLY
CONCEALING HIM.
SHE MUST BE ALL
RIGHT PEOPLE
SAID, OR THE
DUCHESS WOULD
NEVER HAVE SPOKEN
TO HER. SHE WAS
KNOWN IN LONDON
AS "THE WOMAN WITH THE TURQUOISE"
IT CAME AS SUCH A SHOCK TO LONDON
WHEN THE "DAILY MAIL" EXPOSED HER FOR
WHAT SHE WAS.

A page from IDEAS & FANCIES, 1904

no idea that you were one of the house-party, I never noticed you at dinner laſt night.'

He turned round, and to his horror beheld the Duchess of St Andrews.

'Aunt Queenie!' he gasped, and let his spade fall to the ground with a clatter.

'You do not seem quite yourself,' she remarked, 'but why these Tolſtoi habits?' and she pointed to the spade.

'My dear Aunt, you had beſt be told at once,' he said, 'be seated, and prepare yourself for a great shock;' and digging the blade of his spade deep into the soil, he offered her the handle for a chair. 'Be as comfortable as possible,' he hospitably recommended her, 'and remember not to lean back.'

The Duchess opened her parasol. 'I shall have freckles this evening if I remain here long,' she complained, 'so be as quick as you can.'

'Then, dear Aunt, I am Lady Appledore's gardener.'

The Duchess was overcome. 'Oh my spoilt child, that it should have come to this!' she screamed, 'that a nephew of mine . . .' Words failed her. She sought vainly to articulate with her garden gauntlets, the Naſturtiums in her hat shook convulsively, although there was no wind to ſtir them.

'I cannot see, Aunt, what difference it makes to you.'

'Oh! what would your poor-dear-misguided-ambitious mother say now, could she behold you weeding cabbages?' she cried.

'She would be the laſt to blame me. But, dear Aunt, I wish to remain on here, and do not want Lady Appledore to know who I am. Be so good as to say nothing about it.'

The Duchess looked at him in aſtonishment.

'You *wish* to remain here as her gardener?'

'Certainly. Do you know I have never been so happy before. Of course, I dare say I shall give gardening up during the winter, when the weather changes, but these long summer days spent among flowers and fruit charm me beyond words. You have no idea how peaceful my life has been since I arrived at Wiston. No responsibility, nothing to worry about, and all around the good beautiful country, the fresh wild flowers, the free birds, and my friends the trees. Oh, dear Aunt Queenie, do not spoil my happiness.'

'My dearest child, far from it. I am beginning now to think you merely eccentric, and I will even encourage you in your new profession, by presenting you with a complete set of garden tools of your own.'

'My dear, generous Aunt!'

'But tell me,' she went on, 'aren't you a little wee bit in love with Clarida Appledore?'

'Well, then, yes I am,' he admitted, 'and it's just the case of Ruy Blas all over again!'

'I hope not, and I would do my best to help you, but you must see that as long as you are her gardener, it is improper even to think of a wedding. However, come and have tea with me this afternoon, everybody is going to a garden party, so I shall be all alone, and we can talk over everything then.'

'Thanks, Aunt, but you forget the servants. What would Perfect say if he saw us having tea together?'

'Well then, I will tell him to have tea in the Rose Garden. Bring your spade with you, and if anyone comes in sight you can begin to dig. Au revoir.'

* * * * *

'I spent the morning in the garden,' the Duchess said

at lunch. 'What wonderful Roses you have this year, dear, and what a handsome gardener! Where did you get him from?'

'I noticed the man from my bedroom window,' said old Lady Gloria Townley, 'I thought what a perfect footman!'

'Mademoiselle Doucet believes he is an Anarchist,' said Lady Appledore, 'she will not go out on the terrace after twilight, for fear he should murder her.'

'An Anarchist! my nephew an Anarchist! my dear Clarida, what next?'

The Duchess was furious.

'Your nephew, Duchess? What *do* you mean?'

'Oh! how stupid of me to have told you, he doesn't wish it known, but I couldn't hear one of my own blood spoken of as an Anarchist without protesting. However, dear, he *is* my nephew — poor Goda's boy — you know they lost all their money in that horrid coal mine. Still, I believe, Wildred will have about £800 a year, when all the claims are settled, and if he is careful he should be able to manage on that, he is only doing gardening temporarily.'

'This is indeed an interesting young man,' exclaimed the Bishop of Margate, who was one of the party. 'I must try and interview him after lunch for my parochial magazine.'

'We must ask him in to dine with us this evening,' Lady Appledore said. 'Oh! I am so delighted, Duchess, that he is your nephew, I felt all along that he was no *ordinary* gardener.'

'I fell quite in love with him from the bathroom window,' Lady Gloria exclaimed. And then, turning to the Bishop, she suddenly remarked apropos of nothing, 'Oh the tragedy, Bishop, to be called Gloria when one is over sixty!' and she shook her grey curls, and looked away through the open French window, her blue eyes fixed dreamily on the white Peacocks, that stood upon the terrace spreading their tails to the sun.

The Bishop, whose esprit was never very bright after lunch, was mercifully saved making a gallant repartee by Perfect, who tactfully asked him whether he would take Kümmel or Curaçao.

*　　*　　*　　*　　*

Although the stable clock had struck eleven, the night was so bright that he could see to pack without a lamp. The ugly white case stood in the centre of a patch of moonlight, his music and books scattered all around over the uncarpeted floor.

Yes, he was going. How could he stay now that all was known? Had not the Bishop of Margate tried to interview him that afternoon as he was gathering melons for a water ice, and had not Lady Appledore asked him to dinner and music afterwards? Oh! he felt that he would like to strangle the Duchess for her indiscretion.

Tomorrow night he would be back in London again. He had heard from his solicitor that there would be about £800 a year, saved for him out of the débris, but what a shame it was that he could not go on earning Lady Appledore's eighteen-shillings-and-six-pence a week until the end of the summer. He had been so happy at Wiston. He had never been so happy before.

He leaned his arm down on the window-sill, and gazed up at the night.

The sky was glorious with stars, and the moon hung low over the orchard, like a golden apricot on the verge of falling.

The long grass was alight with glow-worms, thousands and thousands of them, so that they appeared to be the reflections of the stars in a still green lake. Hidden amongst the yellow tassels of the Laburnum flower, a bird was telling of all the marvels it had seen across the seas.

'As far as I can understand,' said Wildred, listening, 'she spent last winter in Egypt, with her family; and her youngest daughter, who is very delicate, married a Martin there, and is living in the utmost warmth and comfort in a charming Pyramid, just outside Cairo. This year, she says, she is going to Spain, she longs to visit the Alhambra, and if the Moon will grant her strength of wings, she hopes to fly home by Persia, as she has an invitation to pass a week-end in the Shah's garden: and now,' said Wildred, 'I can no longer understand what she says, but I think she must be doing a serenade by Chaminade.'

The stable clock chimed midnight.

'Hullo! I must get on with my packing,' he murmured, 'but all the same it is not *really* extraordinary that I should be a wee bit in love with Lady Appledore, when the very tiniest bird in the garden has got its mate.'

*　　*　　*　　*　　*

Lady Appledore could not sleep.

She had tried poetry, bromide, and a biographical history of higher Philosophy, and she was still awake.

'It is most extraordinary!' she murmured. 'I suppose it must be the heat.'

She opened her window, and sat there admiring the beauty of the Park at night. 'How wonderful the trees were, and the blue chain of hills beyond, how peaceful!'

'I can so well understand why such numbers of the

Saints flew to the hills,' she told herself, 'I should do exactly the same.'

The scent of flowers rose up from underneath her window—Mignonette, Jasmine, Roses.

'It's no use,' she exclaimed at last, 'I cannot pretend any longer I do not know what's the matter. I love him.'

A peacock floated down from the Cedar tree before the house, and stretched its wings to the first bar of silver light that showed above the woods.

Lady Appledore closed her window.

'You silly woman,' she said to her mirror, 'you will look so plain in the morning after this sleepless night, and it serves you right for being so foolish. He is going away today and doesn't care that for you!'

She took the long pearl ear-rings from her ears, and deposed them for the night on the vellum cover of a Thomas à Kempis.

'Oh! I cannot help it,' she murmured, beginning to sob, 'and I must be natural for once, and as there's no one to see me, it doesn't much matter.'

And spreading herself comfortably on a sofa she indulged in a delicious cry.

*   *   *   *   *

At eight o'clock next morning, when Grantham knocked at Lady Appledore's bedroom door with her cup of chocolate, she was surprised to receive no answer, and still more so when, on entering the room, she did not find her mistress.

'What can have happened?' Grantham wondered, and noticing that the bed had not been slept in, she immediately began to investigate.

'The case looks almost parallel to that of my last poor

mistress,' she murmured, 'where can her ladyship have gone? The nearest creature of prepossessing appearance lives quite half-an-hour's carriage drive away from here, and it would take over three-quarters of an hour to go on foot, and then by taking all the short cuts.'

She picked up a paper-bound French novel, and disapproved of the cover. *L'Amour chez les Turques*, she read.

'I hope her ladyship will not think of going so far as Turkey, the thoughts of a Harem make my blood freeze; and besides, no nice maid likes going further than Paris. When I went to Biarritz last year, and got out at Bayonne by mistake, I thought I should have died.'

She met Alice on the staircase sweeping.

'Have you seen her ladyship?' she inquired.

'Yes, she has gone riding, she passed me half an hour ago, she told me to say she would like breakfast at ten.'

'You are sure she has not been gone more than half an hour?'

'Quite.'

Grantham felt disappointed. Life was so dull in the country, she had hoped that it might have been something a little more exciting.

*   *   *   *   *

Wildred stood on the platform waiting for the train. It was already signalled, but there were five minutes yet before it would start.

The village of Minster-le-Hope appeared over the low white palings of the station, faint and misty as a crayon drawing, in the early morning air.

The grey church tower seemed to exhort the trees about it to grow higher, higher, and the sky above was of such a delicate shade of blue, that it looked as if it had been powdered all over with poudre de riz.

The sound of a horse cantering swiftly broke the silence.

Through the gold broom he caught sight of a woman on horseback.

Could it be? Yes! it was Lady Appledore.

He had never seen her on horseback before. She looked bewitching in her close-fitting habit, and how unusual was the violet pom-pom in her hat!

He ran to meet her.

'Good morning,' he said, 'I am sorry, but I was running away with the key of the Orchid-house on my watch chain, what luck that I should meet you.'

She smiled at him as she took it.

'I wanted to say good-bye to you,' she said. 'I wanted to tell you that . . . that I think it was a very sweet idea of yours to be a gardener! and I hope that we shall often meet again in London. Will you come and see me sometimes in Berkeley Square? You will always be welcome.'

She held out her hand to him.

He took it and kissed it.

'My dear lady,' he said, 'I am sorry to have to leave you. I have been so happy at Wiston, I am afraid I shall never be as happy again, unless' — he broke off — 'Oh promise to write and tell me all about the herbaceous borders, and whether old Bartholomew succeeds in inventing a grey Geranium! You do not know how much all your news will interest me.'

The train was in sight, coming round the bend of the line.

'Good-bye,' she said. 'Good-bye, Mr Forrester.'

'You used to call me Wildred,' he reminded her.

'Ah! that was yesterday — before I knew.'

She kissed her hand to him as the train steamed out of Minster Station, and he waved his hat back to her from his third class carriage.

She remained waving till the train was lost from view.

'Well I never! no! certainly I never did!' exclaimed the station master.

*   *   *   *   *

A year later, on a hot June afternoon, as Mrs Watson the Vicar's wife was returning from her devotions, she happened to meet Mrs Massey, the new châtelaine of Cheapthorpe Priory.

Mrs Massey was the rich wife of a Bond Street jeweller.

'Her ear-rings are almost more trying to the eyes than the sun,' was Mrs Watson's reflection as she opened her parasol.

'Good morning,' Mrs Massey said, 'am I late for Church?'

She was a small woman, faultlessly dressed in a linen gown by Worth, her pyramid of bright red hair was an exact match of the Water Naiad's in Henner's picture at the Luxembourg.

'Yes, service is over,' Mrs Watson told her. 'Today is the festival of St Enias.'

'Was not St Enias before his conversion the husband of an Italian girl who danced the Tarantella?' asked Mrs Massey, who loved gossip, 'or am I thinking of somebody else?'

As Mrs Watson had never heard of the Tarantella she spoke of the Vicar's health.

'He is frightfully overworked,' she complained, 'and in our small parish, you will hardly credit it, there are no fewer than three widowed peeresses, and a wounded general.'

'A wounded general!' exclaimed Mrs Massey, 'how pathetic!'

'He lives in the big white house you can see through the trees. They never found the bullet.'

'Poor lingering man! But do you think, Mrs Watson, that he would care to come to tea, if I wrote a nice little note and asked him?'

'My dear, he never leaves his couch,' Mrs Watson informed her. 'The Vicar sometimes goes and reads to him, but he does not seem to listen, just goes on playing with his toy soldiers, exterminating Dervishes that his housekeeper buys for him in boxes in the village.'

'I will send him a case of real good ones from the Stores,' said Mrs Massey, much moved, 'but tell me, Mrs Watson, who lives in that red Victorian-looking house?'

'It's Elizabethan,' Mrs Watson informed her, 'and belongs to Mrs Wildred Forrester. You must have heard of her as Lady Appledore. Poor Lord Appledore! such a good man! such a staunch Protestant! so different from his frivolous wife! Her second marriage was disgraceful, the Vicar refused to marry them, so they had to go to Knightsbridge. Why, my dear Mrs Massey, I have *seen* Mr Forrester come round to the Vicarage back door with a basket of Seakale! Of course when she married him she tried to get people to believe he was well connected. Said he was a nephew of the Duchess of St Andrews, and a cousin of *the* Forresters. But whatever the relationship *may* have been, I feel thoroughly convinced that it has not been properly renewed since the days of Noah.'

Mrs Massey looked bewildered. 'But who was her husband?' she inquired.

'You may well ask; and you will scarcely believe me when I tell you that Lady Appledore married her gardener!'

Mrs Massey stood still, and clutched at Mrs Watson's arm for support.

'I never heard of such a mésalliance,' she gasped.

FIN

The New Rythum

by
RONALD FIRBANK

THE NEW RYTHUM

I

IT WAS a pink and elusive evening towards the break of Easter. Zephyr and Flora caressed New York, yearned above her glimmering parks and gardens, brooded above her budding avenues (awakening young chestnut-leaf and drowsy lilac), rippled that way, this way, all caprice, eventually cutting an elfin caper with the night above the aloof façade of Mr Harry Rosemerchant's residence on Riverside.

Lolling in an immense camphor-coloured car before the door, Lionel, the very young, very blond, and very dissipated-looking chauffeur, felt his ambitions rise. To have won stardom as a Boxer! Worshipped by all New York: 'My little Lionel, I love you': and then, some soft-voiced Venus, perhaps, to twine her arms about him: 'I love you, I love you.'

He rolled an eye upward towards the loggia full of flowers. Sometimes a blossom would open, bloom, and perish while Mrs Rosemerchant changed her gown.

One long white blind down captured sensitively, as he gazed, a fleeting silhouette.

'Heigh-ho, I guess it's one of her peacock nights,' he exclaimed, directing a smile at the mounting moon; 'top-knot feathers mean late hours!'

Pecking at a magazine, while a maid dressed her hair,

Mrs Harry Rosemerchant (née Catherine Cornabilt) seemed disposed to loiter.

'Shall it be brilliants, madam?'

'It shall.'

'The diadem or the cross, madam?'

'Oh, shut up.'

Mrs Rosemerchant addressed a pianola that was playing a remote Hawaiian air beside her.

All susceptibility and egotism, the domestic stiffened: 'A maid has her feelings, madam!'

'What about them?'

'I wish to give warning!'

'Don't be a touchy fool and stop that infernal noise,' Mrs Rosemerchant enjoined, continuing with nonchalance her journal. From the glowing headlines it appeared a singularly hectic number. 'Fifth Av. Scandal,' she read, 'New York's New Vice: Society Women Birched With Roses. Multi-millionairess Whipped With Thorns. Widow Of Defunct Senator Mandarin-Dove Declares For *Gloire de Dijon* While Mrs Culling Browne Says Dorothy Perkins Are Best.'

'I wonder?' She turned a page and paused, arrested by a laughing portrait of a girl: 'Winner of the All America Beauty Prize, and perhaps one of the loveliest women in existence — Miss Dreadfuline Hancock of Bloody Brook, Mass.'

'Gee. She's terribly handsome.' Mrs Rosemerchant fetched a breath.

It was a face of a wayward, Renaissance type, exciting enthusiasm and admiration — it was evident from the votes — almost equally from her own sex as from men.

'Your rope and cross, madam.'

'. . . My what?'

'Your diamonds, madam!'

'Take those away; and give me my Eros instead,' Mrs Rosemerchant directed, dwelling dreamfully on the radiant portrait. It appeared the charming child was too confused and elated by her good fortune at obtaining the prize to say more to the press than: 'Five hundred and fifty dollars . . .! What shall I do with it all, oh I feel bewildered.'

'Exquisite kitten!' Mrs Rosemerchant rippled, mistaking a jade unguent jar on the toilet-table for the candy.

She surveyed seraphically her reflected image with half-closed glittering eyes: the Cornabilt nose, piquant, devil-may-careish, and determined, slightly masculine lips and chin; the slim Madonna neck, supporting heavy gold-burnished locks, that seemed to shed, somehow, the halo of money. 'Ah, darling.' A tender sigh escaped her.

'One of the small quiver stones is loose, madam!'

'Hell.'

'Madam?'

'You prick me!'

Wondering how certain women could inject themselves for fun (poor little Fanny Lowensohn *née* Newdirty of New Orleans for instance was perpetually prodding herself with a great horrid needle), Mrs Rosemerchant repaired in anticipation of, perhaps, a cocktail towards her husband's dressing-room.

'Harry?'

From the articles on the bed he was apparently not yet home.

'It's naughty of him how he slaves,' she reflected, lifting his evening trousers to her cheek; their slight, provocative fragrance recalled the pinkish Poinciana-flowers around Palm Beach: 'Great giant, I love you,' she murmured, turning in some confusion at a sound of muffled merriment behind her.

Squatting on the floor she beheld a young negro dependent of the house.

'O Lord my God!' the niggerling evoked Him.

'Eh?'

'I swear by all de church spires ob New York city — by all dose church spires I take no more dan three drops; sh'o, surtainly! Den yo' come in an' rub y'u cheek to Misteh Rosemerchant's trews an' dat just staht me laffin'.'

'Little savage, be gone,' Mrs Rosemerchant exclaimed: to be surprised, unawares, in a primitive gesture, was decidedly vexing.

'Sh'o Mass' Harry he dat han'some, I could kiss his pants meself.'

'Enough!'

'An' I'd do de same to any ob de fambly.'

Mrs Rosemerchant unbent a shade. English butlers and French maids, as rueful experience teaches, are apt to be less devoted. 'You're just a baby, Co-co,' she said, 'with a big Southern heart. Good night!'

Descending to a boudoir, a little quiet room with a sense of harvest, Mrs Rosemerchant resumed equably the vivacious news-sheet: 'Virginia Beach Scandal: Member Of Seawanhaka Yacht Club Arrested In A Boarding House Near Grammercy Park: "I did not do it," he exclaims coolly as detectives seized him.' And there again was the enchanting Dreadfuline.

'The magnifier'; she peered about her for a strong-lens, and preoccupied forgot it. It was too bad of Harry to be detained downtown, she reflected, gathering up from her escritoire a black-bordered invitation card. *Bertie Waldorf at Home: 'To watch me have a tooth drawn'.*

'Let's pray it's not his wisdom!' she sighed, drifting
moodily to the piano. A 'Berceuse in Z', a waltz, 'His
Lips' (then at the height of the vogue), and some 'Variations on a Sex Theme' lay scattered upon it. Opening
petulantly the Variations, she attacked *con fuoco* an intri-
cate passage. The emotional dual rhythm (replete in
subtlest shades and rich recourse) required no small tech-
nique. Playing with delicate adroitness, she glanced
about her. Five hundred thousand dollars for one of his
hard-coaxed dreams — her eyes swept a modern canvas
suspended on the wall. A sombre and baffling bit of
brushwork. 'Oh I feel bewildered'; the words of Miss
Hancock, recurring to mind, caused her to titter. 'Exquisite kitten,' she murmured, focusing some sceptres of
growing hyacinths beside her that filled all the air with
sweetness. Diverging, insensibly, into the adagio, her
agile fingers wandered on. 'Delicious the introspective
parts,' she breathed, regarding through the parted cur-
tains the large and radiant stars.

'Remember, dearest, not all that is interesting to play
is interesting to hear!' Mr Rosemerchant, as he bent to
kiss her neck, made the quiet observation.

'Oh, Harry.'

'After an active day I protest against such musical
dyspepsia.'

'Oh, Harry?' Her gaze travelled slowly over him: dark
bullet head, touched with grey; intelligent, slightly
womanish eyes; the prettiest little, most cherished little,
black moustache imaginable, shadowing perfectly chiselled
lips.

'Have you forgotten it's tonight, dear, we're asked to
witness Bertie Waldorf's tooth drawn?'

Mr Rosemerchant consulted casually a clock.

'Well; I guess it'll be out by now.'

'There will probably be dancing, dear, afterwards. In fact I know he has engaged Victor Fisher's Blue-of-Blues Jazz Band.'

With a short expletive he dropped to her day-bed, heaped with lace pillows stuffed with violets.

Mortified, she made as if to rise, then struck a wistful chord in silence — an indolent husband, a neglected wife.

' "Deceived Countess Hurls Hot Potato At Betrothed And Bolts From Downtown Supper-club",' he was perusing the glaring headlines of the periodical upon the couch.

'Say-y, dearest, hustle, do.'

' "Winner of the All America Beauty Prize and perhaps" — '

In fluttered alacrity she rose and came towards him: 'Oh Harry . . . Don't you think she is, dear . . . *rather* sweet?'

'Mnps; type Bar Bedaan, Thessalonica Lounge,' he commented.

'Oh Harry.'

'Some vixen.'

'———— . . . ?' her eyelids quivering worked.

' "I bequeath",' he was beginning to regale her in mellifluous tones with the account of The Suicide of an Artist: ' "I bequeath my sad disgusted heart to the Hospitals." '

'Well, I'm willing mine away too, you know.'

'Sweetheart, to me?'

'Go and change, Harry, and never mind,' she bade him.

Humming a little pensive air beneath her breath she wandered about the room. Although a consummate dearest, it was a trifle trying how Harry would bring everything down to dust: 'I suppose it's just his nature,' she reflected, fingering an ormolu paper-weight on her bureau, in the shape of the outstretched claws of a beast; it was a gift from the oil-king Otto van Cotton. It served to remind her she must come to a decision on her gown for a forthcoming fancy-ball, everyone to go as animals.

'I almost think a butterfly, no a firefly, no a wasp,' she deliberated, sinking to a fauteuil of rose-coloured satin: 'something light and wingy . . . I could never go as a rabbit or a dog; though as a squirrel, perhaps, I might! . . . Still, *not* a tail . . . I could not assume a tail. Peacocks, of course, they had them; but peacocks, bewitching things, were birds. 'A bird?' she raised her eyes for inspiration to a summer landscape by Daubigny, 'a bird might do, though nothing native. . . . Something for choice exotic. A cockatoo for instance . . .' She sought a pen and commenced a tentative design: 'but no: on the whole, a butterfly, I believe, would suit me more; tropic, and with about the amount of drapery one would display off Coronado Beach. . . .'

Humming airily, she conceived a few fanciful designs, surpassing Nature boldly in improvising venturesome festoons and falling streamers. Hadn't vixens, too, got wings? In Japan there were flying foxes . . . *there* would be a costume, now, that no one else would have. Probably a dozen women or more would turn up as moths and butterflies, but a flying fox . . .

'I guess I'll be a flying fox!' She made a soaring movement heavenward with her hands. 'But for Harry's horrid criticism of Miss Hancock, it would have hardly occurred to me,' she told herself, toying restlessly with the Eros on her gown. She smiled, transported by a sudden idea, her physiognomy passing from languor to languor. Then impulsively changing her pen, she wrote:

'Dear Child,

Should you by chance be contemplating a little trip to New York, call on me, do, at 2 Riverside. I want to see you.'

II

Having nibbled a cake at Sherry's, and left a card in Madison Avenue on the Archbishop of New York (who was yet again, it seemed, a father), Mrs. Rosemerchant told Lionel to drop her beneath the elm trees in Central Park. Turning into Fifty-ninth Street, however, she altered her mind, and directed him to a house on Fifth Avenue a little beyond the synagogue. Skirting the Park, enchanting now, decked in the very first earliest buds of spring, the car slackened speed before an edifice in brown stone, constructed on the lines of a château François Ier.

Assembling simultaneously in a batch together several equipages were obstructing the roadway just ahead. Blocking her windscreen, she recognized Bertie Waldorf's handsome English horses of Tetrarch grey, with their white and silver harness, and the closed limousine of Mrs Stella Mandarin Dove. Evidently the committee of the Animals Subscription-ball in aid of the 'Ada Beamish Maternity-home Extension' was rallying loyally to the president, Mrs Otto van Cotton.

'It's remarkable always how Selina can compel attendance,' Mrs Rosemerchant reflected, alighting between a couple of smiling Sphinxes, bearing a monogram and the device: *Take Nature as it comes.*

Following leisurely in the wake of several vanishing backs, she found herself beneath a Renaissance rotunda, bare but for an antique statue or two, and a vast black fan in magnificent mosaics that comprised the floor: from the adjoining reception rooms came a convivial hum of voices.

Repudiating Birth-control, believing that men and women should multiply and increase, the 'Ada Beamish' appeal found in Mrs Van Cotton an ideal supporter.

An altercation over the choice of cotillion favours was in progress as Mrs Rosemerchant was announced.

'For the fifth figure let us provide vanity bags for the gentlemen and moustache-brushes for the ladies,' a bald, clean-shaven man in horn-rimmed glasses had just launched the suggestion.

'Give me to know, Baron, which favour goes to which?'

'Say everybody, why not whips?' The proposal fell from the lips of a woman of almost fearsome beauty, recalling Medusa, with her long trembling ear-rings and dark-parted hair.

'First give me to know, dear, what we all would do with them? . . . ? . . . ?'

Welcomed rapturously by her hostess, Mrs Rose-merchant lost the reply.

Benefactress, arbitress, patroness, wielding inter-national influence, Mrs Otto van Cotton was a striking example of a well-ordered mind in a well-ordered body, the four orbs of her figure being proportioned equally— before and behind. In a state of joyous ferment, the news had come but some few moments back that her daughter, the Duchess of Valdivia, was shortly returning with her husband from Europe to the States bringing with them something that would set all America talking.

'Mercy, Selina, what can it be?'

'Well, I really daren't tell you yet; and that's the true truth, dear,' Mrs Van Cotton declared, her eyes wandering to Bertie Waldorf who was standing in idle adoration before a statue.

'Your beautiful things are almost paralysing, Mrs Van Cotton,' he murmured blandly turning.

'Well, I sincerely hope not,' she exclaimed, ogling the marble shape of an Apollo, assigned to Ortisthenes, the Greek.

'It's peculiar the perfect film-faces folk had in the year dot!'

'Is that so?' she answered, shooting an oblique glance at the mole on his third blue chin.

Something of a dilettante, he was said to be editing *The Glory-book of Complaisant Husbands*, with portraits of thirty-two gentlemen in medallions inset.

A round of applause from the seated committee caused a fleeting diversion.

Carried away by philanthropic fervour, a little woman, arrayed in slightly fatigued mourning, softly pressed 'New York's richest bachelor's' arm: 'I want you to make a date with me, Bertie, for one of my Friendly Evenings.'

Believing in the evolution of the Negro, the Friendly Evenings arranged for them by Mrs Stella Mandarin Dove (in which spiced buns and other belly munition would be devoured) were somewhat variously viewed.

Detecting in a far-off corner the magnificent abdomen of the Reverend Cedric Potts, Mrs Rosemerchant made towards him. Looking like iceless butter in August, he was descanting, with the graces of a screen-favourite, to Iris Iquiavi, the poetess, whose polished verse perhaps accounted for her face half massaged away.

'How you did lay on, Father, Sunday, at St Pat's! I was there both times,' Mrs Rosemerchant murmured sweetly swimming up.

'Come and hear me next week at All Saints!' *Come and hear me next week at the New Amsterdam*: a popular actor might have employed just such similar tones.

The poetess shuddered: 'I'll be riding the waves I expect then,' she said, '*en route* for France and England!'

'Somehow I've no desire much to visit England. I seem to know what it's like.'

'I'm told London in Spring is terribly relaxing.'

'Well, so long as it's no worse!' the poetess answered, considering with a supercilious eye Raphael's *Madonna with a hoe*, an exquisite variation of *La Belle Jardinière* in the Paris Louvre.

'I doubt you'll find in the old world choicer old masters than are here in this house,' Father Potts observed, bestowing a tender look on Longhi's triumphal portrait of the Venetian courtezan *Donna Leila Lin*.

A remark a mild little man with the minimum of expression chanced to hear.

'That may be so, and probably is,' he chuckled, chafing equably the palms of his hands.

Nothing rejoiced the master of the house more than to hear his treasures extolled: 'Come and see our boys and girls in stone!' he would sometimes unostentatiously invite a stranger to view his private Gallery. Accompanied by an Englishwoman, the Hon. Mrs Edward Facile-Manners, who was new, it seemed, to New York, he had just concluded a tour through the beautiful chandeliered apartments.

'Selina has been telling me of your daughter's return.'

'Yes, she sails in the *Berengaria*.'

'Let us hope in time for the ball . . .'

It was with an heroic sense of duty accomplished that Mrs Rosemerchant found herself back in the car.

'Round Harlem Mere,' she directed Lionel.

It was the hour when the lilac downsoaring shadows begin to lengthen towards the South, and the Western sky recalls mint sterling.

Speeding along in her cosy car, the utter hush of luxury, Mrs Rosemerchant abandoned herself to reverie.

All a-shimmer in the early dusk, Croton Reservoir surpassed in exuberance the costliest Tiffany tiara, set in the emerald meadows beyond. Calcined against its glitter, she caught the laughing silhouette of Laura Shymoon of the Ziegfeld Follies trotting her notorious pink-nosed ponies and, flitting on, glimpsed the purpurine plague of Harlem Mere. Returning via the Mall, she turned, charmed by a pink horse-chestnut tree just breaking into flower.

Cornelius the footman and Potter the butler were in readiness at 2 Riverside to aid her alight.

'There's a young lady from Massachusetts, 'm, waiting to see you,' the senior servant announced.

'From *Massachusetts*?'

'Miss Dreadfuline Hancock; come from Bloody Brook, 'm.'

III

'Darling, I want to call you by some other name than Dreadfuline. Let me call you Heliodora.'

'Call me just anything, dear, you choose to; I guess it's real sweet of you to care.'

The proposal was made by Mrs Rosemerchant a few days later, immediately following lunch.

Things from the first had advanced with singular velocity and rush; almost, indeed, by flashes.

'You know I never could rest satisfied with your name.'

'N . . . o?'

'No.'

'Heliodora!'

'Ora Dora Iodora Eliodora Heliodora. Heavenly, isn't it?'

They were seated in the short stretch of garden attached to the Rosemerchant residence like some leafy saloon tête-à-tête.

The society of perhaps the loveliest woman in existence was as revivifying, Mrs Rosemerchant fancied, as some perfect tango, or an ocean-breeze off Narragansett Pier.

'Well, it's real sweet of you, I reckon, to offer me this wonderful time.'

'Dear child, why I've done nothing whatever for you, yet,' Mrs Rosemerchant answered, focusing the trim form of Co-co, who presented himself with a card; scanning it, she read: 'Sadie Crow. (Espionage) Publicity'.

'De lady waitin'!'

'Deny her.'

'An' Misteh Waldorf at de telephone, 'm, to know if he find you in lateh?'

'Deny him, too.'

With a dozen conflicting rumours of a new and sensational beauty come to town, visits of curiosity were bound to be expected. It was but natural that social arbiters should hanker to participate in a so intriguing discovery; should scramble for the satisfaction of being the first to sponsor or deride, encourage or condemn.

'Don't drive them all away, dear, will you,' Miss Hancock begged, twirling a freckled Iris in a hand that was perhaps enlarged a little by manual labour.

Mrs Rosemerchant raised smiling eyes into the brightness of the sky.

'I wish I could!'

'That's because you're spoiled, dear, and have corn to scatter.'

'Corn to scatter?'

'Money to burn.'

'Money; why money's nothing once you've got it.'

'Exactly.'

Mrs Rosemerchant looked detached.

'Since the rain,' she observed, 'it's just as though fairies had been at work.'

'Spring up in Bloody Brook comes late; later than it does here; usually there are no new potatoes or green peas before they're half over in Boston.'

'You surprise me, dear child!' Mrs Rosemerchant murmured, starting the gramophone: after a shower she enjoyed dancing with naked feet on the warm green of the grass.

'I just love the Isolde cocktail music from *Tristan*, when it's jazzed, don't you?'

'I never know one Opera, darling, from another. Isn't that the one with Fricka's rams?'

They had been bobbing and dipping, gliding and running, clasping and parting, swaying and turning together some time, when Cornelius announced Mrs Otto van Cotton.

'Damn.'

'She is in the Library, 'm.'

'Perfect idiot.'

Leaving Heliodora to a forlorn *pas de seule*, Mrs Rose-merchant repaired within.

It was inevitable that Mrs Van Cotton with her wide experience and flair should be among the earliest to call.

The 'Library', a feather summery room (containing scarcely six books), was remarkable chiefly for Sargent's masterly study of *Lesbia Lukewarm*.

She found Mrs Van Cotton looking big, handsome and vague in a gown of mouse-grey velvet and a turban wreathed in blossoms.

'Sel — ina . . .!' with a little cry, expressive of bright surprise, Mrs Rosemerchant skimmed towards her.

Being on the water-front it had been impossible, it seemed, to go by — Mrs Van Cotton sketched a supple gesture, suited to a mother-in-law of a Latin duke.

'You must be getting wild to see Pauline,' Mrs Rose-merchant said, sinking to a *causeuse* by her side.

The Duchess of Valdivia's return to the States with a Greek marble of the Golden Age, none other than Praxiteles' long lost 'Hercules with a fearsome bottom', from the god's great temple at Eleusis and acquired by Mr Otto van Cotton at a colossal figure above the heads of the whole of art-competing Europe, was the subject of universal press-excitement and comment.

'The necessary Government formalities, I fear, may delay her; in which case, I shouldn't wonder if she remained for Longchamps and Ascot,' Mrs Van Cotton replied.

'Americans abroad say she's terribly much admired.'

Mrs Van Cotton coughed discreetly.

'All New York is chattering, dear, of the young creature who graced your box at the Metropolitan the other night.'

'Oh?'

'Tell me, Nellie; who is she, what is she?' Mrs Van Cotton wheezed a little.

Mrs Rosemerchant smiled nervously.

'I gather,' she said, 'she is gently born; but you may as well know, Selina — and the child herself is proud of it — she was once a laundress.'

'A laundry-hand? Impossible.'

'Just that.'

'I pray to God, dear, you are not making a social mistake,' Mrs Van Cotton impressively said, ogling obliquely the Sargent on the wall.

'Well, I suppose she's not the first in the States, Selina, to have had humble beginnings. . . .'

'Has she no talents at all to recommend her?'

Mrs Rosemerchant blossomed into smiles.

'Some of her laundry mishaps, Selina; oh, they're so droll!'

Mrs Van Cotton fixed her attention on a passing pleasure-boat through the window.

'You live out on Riverside — right off the beat; you defy the conventions,' she said, shaking her head.

'I dare say, Selina, we shall never create a vogue for the Hudson, but Heliodora is another matter,' Mrs Rosemerchant rippled, as a trim trio of menservants appeared with refreshment.

Being due however at a wedding in the Crystal Room at the Ritz-Carlton, Mrs Van Cotton was unable to linger.

Favouring a strawberry with the pressure of her lips, she braced herself, sighed and rose.

'Society! It's a vocation,' she pronounced, ambling majestically on her long wand-like cane over the parquet flooring.

'And a highly strenuous one!' Mrs Rosemerchant laughed, following her forth to the hall.

Fixing an early dinner-date to meet the new beauty, Mrs Van Cotton drove away.

Caressing amatively her pearls, and humming, beneath her breath, a little air of joy, Mrs Rosemerchant returned to the garden.

IV

That the *Berengaria*, bearing to the new world the very apple of Pagan art, should break her record and be sighted off Sandy Hook just as the curtain was rising at the Metropolitan Opera-house on the world première of *Paphos*, was socially if not nautically a regrettable error. Regarded by the Intelligentsia as an informal National event, the arrival of the Prax Herc, the World's Greatest Nude, simultaneously with the *Paphos* première, created an artistic clash, an excess of brilliance bordering upon plethora. Indeed, a fluttered galleryite, torn in two to assist at the historic landing and to applaud Frau Eva Montazah in the rôle of Venus, found an outlet to surfeited feelings by being gently ill into space, to the indignation of a section of the stalls.

Seated in her habitual parterre box, with the composer at her side, Mrs Van Cotton was on thorns. To leave the good man alone in glory without offending him beyond all hope of pardon, would require strategy, *savoir faire*: 'Well, if it's not some warm,' she murmured, ogling his blond beard, and wielding with lethargy her fan.

She was looking almost girlish draped in Byzantine white with Aaron's prophetic stones Urim and Thummim, set by Cartier, on her head: 'If it's not some close,' she reiterated, taking up an opera-glass and levelling it at the house.

A more remarkable gathering was seldom seen.

Manipulating the lenses she espied, in the grand tier among the assiduous faithful, Mr and Mrs Dupont J. Hoppin and their débutante daughter 'Joy', a bustless, hipless, chinless little thing, Senator and Mrs Elmer Theus Tuesday (she, decked in diamonds and honest rolls of silver fat), while craning from the neighbouring box, in a state of drowsy inertia, Mrs Fanny Lowensohn, *née* Newdirty of New Orleans, with a complexion of the colour of canned apricots, appeared to be expecting a pigeon with cocaine. Dropping the optic to the stalls, she grew aware of the Hon. Edward Facile-Manners in bright attendance on Laura Shymoon of the Ziegfeld Follies, and, conspicuous, close by, Bertie Waldorf and an ultra-elegant youth, both agitating their opera-glasses re-proachfully at someone in the direction of the roof. Deciding to leave the theatre on the score of faintness, Mrs Van Cotton was about to 'come over queer', when a summons from the diva behind called the composer away.

Waving comprehensively her fan, she conveyed to her acquaintance that she was for the counter-attraction.

A moon far gone, and casting a pensive halo, was looking down on Broadway.

It was a perfect night.

Finding no ready coin in her pochette (as, indeed, is not infrequent at all of an evening with ladies), she re-warded the page who procured the car with a condescend-ing slap on the cheek with her cheque-book, and directed the chauffeur to the docks.

TRINITY HALL SPORTS AT CAMBRIDGE.

Although frost had made the path hard, good sport was witnessed at Cambridge on Monday and yesterday, when the Trinity Hall sports took place. (1) The start for the one mile race, which was won easily by E. Oliver. (2) V. G. Thew, the football Blue, wins the quarter-mile race in 53 3-5s. (3) F. Trenchard winning the high jump with a jump of 5ft. (4) C. Tacon wins the putting-the-weight contest with a throw of 32ft. 1½in. —(*Daily Mirror* photographs.)

Page 8 from the Daily Mirror *of February 5th, 1908. The fourth starter from the left in the top picture is Ronald Firbank*

A view of Firbank's room at Trinity Hall, Cambridge, 1907

Another view of the same

RONALD
FIRBANK
*on a Nile
house-boat,
no date*

Turning along Thirty-ninth Street the car passed into Seventh Avenue.

It was the hour when ring-eyed travellers from the violet South emerge from the Central Terminus to be caught up in the great nocturnal pleasure-stream of New York. Driving exuberant citizens from the bright-lit restaurants, dandy mechanics, holding some one word tight in their linnet-heads — Astor? Belasco? Criterion? Hackett? — must here slacken down, often only for a battered taxi-cab or a common lorry.

Ruminating on the *Berengaria*'s arbitrary behaviour (it looked almost as though the captain would be a young man, with a wife, or mistress, with whom he wished to pass an extra night), Mrs Van Cotton caressed absently the folds of her mantle of green cloth of gold: anyway, it would be nice to see Pauline, and the new French frocks . . .

Perhaps the Duchess of Valdivia's Paris hats and *lingerie* (were the whole truth told) rejoiced her heart more than any statue or any painting that ever had crossed the Atlantic.

Musing comfortably on this and that, she observed that the car had gained Thirteenth Street, from whence, traversing Eighth Avenue, it diverged into dreary Horatio Street, startling two men chatting beneath the mauve mystery of a wall.

For the convenience of representatives of the Fine Arts, and a host of others, invited to witness the debarkation of *The World's Greatest Nude*, Mr Otto van Cotton, in his habitual splendid way, had caused to be erected by the wharfside a beflagged marquee, open upon one side to the halcyon breeze. Arriving on the heels of the Lieutenant-Governor and the Mayor of the Borough of

Bronx, Mrs Van Cotton pressed gamely after them through a crowd of ubiquitous telegraph-messengers, express men and softly grinning darkie boys.

'I am assured,' the Lieutenant-Governor archly asserted as they entered the marquee: 'I am assured it puts the Farnese Hercules to the blush!'

With an ability to organize, under difficulties, akin to genius, Mr Van Cotton had surpassed himself now; few but he could have secured, at such brief warning, the professional services of Mrs Julia Portland Stone, the distinguished classic actress, or have induced Demetrias, the Hellenic dancer, to expound by the wharfside the magic of her art.

A gathering composed variously of celebrities in high finance and young married women (all agog to form an opinion of the Greek god's parts) were revolving about a cold buffet, where a popular journalist, familiar to millions by the name of 'One Who Knows', was proclaiming Mr Van Cotton to be a 'Mycaenas', which, with his peculiar enunciation, sounded to some ears (including those of Mrs Van Cotton) like *Mighty Ass*. Glancing around, she was about to exchange a polite word with Sir Joseph Duveen as an examining officer approached with the news that the Duke of Valdivia and his duchess (if not actually the Herc) were liable to be detained on Ellis Island through neglect of formalities.

'I guess my daughter's no alien, sir; and her father I reckon will tell you the same,' Mrs Van Cotton alleged, turning an outraged eye on Mrs Portland Stone, who had commenced recapturing the Past with an excerpt from *Iphigenia in Aulis*.

But with high officialdom at hand over-zealous subordinates were promptly put to rout. With deserters from

the Opera-house arriving one after another in rapid succession, the scene by the wharf was growing increasingly
lively.

'Little white snow-flake, see here!' A big bodied
darkie boy (possessed of a voice quite full of sun) was
emboldened to accost Miss Joy Hoppin and a débutante
friend.

'Young man: I guess you're asking to get lynched!'
they yapped together.

With a wild cry, alarming to the nerves of a waiter
serving contraband brandy in a teacup, the eminent
actress brought the excerpt from Euripides to a close.

Nibbling a cheese sandwich, with much quiet relish,
Mr Van Cotton (who had not yet dined) was prattling
'Wall Street' with Baron Drenkmann of Vienna.

'Bunkum and poppycock, believe me, Baron, nothing
but blandee and swank,' he affirmed, focusing the harbour
lights beyond the white wood-pecker profile of 'One
Who Knows'.

'Well, I'll be damned, man! You don't say?' the
Baron marvelled, opening his old eyes mazy with
money.

'Gee, but I do!' Mr Van Cotton twittered, turning to
congratulate Mrs Julia Portland Stone.

'It reminds me some of the tent in *Monna Vanna*, the
actress anounced, waving a bouquet of ruby-leaved roses
at the wind-stirred canvas. Beyond the flag-fringed doorway the dark sky loomed strewn with long veins of
whitest cloud.

A distant hoot, followed by a stampede of dock-hands,
proclaimed the *Berengaria*.

To the refrain of *The Star-Spangled Banner*, and a ringing
cheer for the master marble that had withstood Time's

onslaught two thousand springtides (slow, honied springs of Greece), the impatient liner hove to shore.

Stationed beneath the awning, looking like some Queen of Golconda, Mrs Van Cotton, flashing Urim and Thummim, awaited her own. Ogling the passengers as they tripped down the great ship's side, she identified the dolled-up features of Violet Countess of Sprotborough, the venerable Bishop of London (as ugly as a gargoyle of a bad school), and old Sir Leonard Needleman, who had come over, it was believed, to look for an heiress. Behind the beer-barrel form of the prelate, a white and radiant figure was blowing kisses, kisses, kisses. . . .

'There she is!'

Preceding the famous statue, and pursued by a bevy of eager reporters, the Duchess fell weeping and laughing on her mother's neck: 'Oh, boy! It's *some* behind!' she brokenly fluted.

'Well; if it's anything in proportion to the price Papa paid! . . .' Mrs Van Cotton exclaimed, embracing her daughter dearly.

Following his wife, squeaking '*Vive* America', '*Vive* Dollarland', ambled the Duke of Valdivia with a favourite dog — a fine brood matron Police.

'Freddie, why-y —— !!'

A domestic scene of international social interest — recorded by innumerable cameras — was interrupted brusquely by Mrs Portland Stone; mistaking her Grace's great dress-basket for the divinity's draped shape, she burst forth into a paean of welcome:

'Fearsome of buttocks, broad of breast, Hail Hercules, son of Amphitryon of Argos!'

A mortifying miscarriage which was to cost her her friendship with the author.

Descending from the skies, as all gods should, the veiled colossus (escorted by detectives and insurance men) in due course was swung ashore.

Coming up at the crucial moment, Mrs Rosemerchant with her Heliodora joined the devout processional to the tent.

'But indeed, indeed, dear; naked men do not please me,' Miss Hancock was saying.

'Tell me, dearest, have you ever seen one?'

'No. Yes. Lots. At Bloody Brook bathing . . .'

Amid tributes of bay and laurel from the 'Eleusis Society', the 'Friends of Ganymede', and a wreath of cup-like, waxen flowers from the 'Disciples of Sappho', the glory of the Golden Age was set reverently down.

A brief causerie upon the art of Praxiteles, as contrasted with modern American tendencies and ideals, brought the unveiling of the masterpiece to an issue.

'Oh!'

With its look of Nick Tickell, the boxer, there was an exclamation of surprise.

It was Nick; Nick to the very life; without his breeches.

'Gosh, if it ain't our Boy!'

'Oh, sweetie Mrs Rosemerchant! . . .' With an incalculable sigh, Miss Hancock sought her mentor's hand.

Stupendous: both the Directors of the Corcoran Gallery, Washington, and of the Metropolitan Museum were unanimous.

'I'll own,' Mr Van Cotton wistfully said, 'I'll own I kind of regret it ain't a she.'

'A what, sir?'

'A she, sir; I guess I'd rather have had a nymph . . .'

'We must take Nature as it comes, sir; remember your

device,' the Lieutenant-Governor exclaimed, regarding the dancer Demetrias silhouetted with arms of brass against the night.

Ignoring the curious glances and the impertinent stares of the young examining-officers on the wharf (are not our armpits as Nature made them?), the foreign artist evoked proud Eleusis and the Punic Wars.

'Vrai; elle est épatante,' the Duchess declared.

But a report that an idol had just arrived and was being adored with heathen rites had reached the Salvation Army: advancing along the quay to the refrain of *Mary of Minnesota*, they came upon the scene just as the dancer prostrated herself to Artemis at the Fearsome's feet.

For once, it seemed, Rumour had not lied: Report had not exaggerated.

'Say, Sister; are you saved?' A growing boy of fifteen with magnificent eyes aboarded Mrs Van Cotton.

'Come on with me to Jesus now!' a negress with a tambourine and big blue bonnet cajoled the duke.

The desire however to hear something of the last act at the Metropolitan was taking many stall and box-holders back to Broadway.

Dispersing to the strains of a salvationist hymn, society soon was scattered.

Towering aloof above its guardians, the white colossus awaited transport with the dawn.

'Fingers five by three, phallus ten by eight; restored . . .' An insurance-officer was conscientiously verifying that all was as it should be.

'They was masterful chaps in them days; eh mates?' a wharf-watchman dormitively observed.

'Abdomen slightly discoloured': absorbed in statistics the agent deafly pursued.

'No exactly one of your moral sort from the look of
'im!'

'Posterior — chipped in two places.'

'Wasn't the old boy a lover of Helen of Troy?'

'Torso damaged.'

'Heigh-ho; I guess he's seen some service!'

'Plinth — Parian, pink — polish gone.'

The investigations over, the men seated themselves
quietly side by side before their charge. Across the
deserted landing-stage the fitful lightning waxed and
waned and through pale sprays of cloud familiar Venus
glimmered brightly.

v

'Oh, sweetie Mrs Rosemarchant, why mercy, what a big
one; mine you see's quite small!'

They had been invited to pick strawberries, 'Tea to
pick strawberries' at the house of Bertie Waldorf on
Upper Park Avenue, and were comparing baskets. One
of a pleasant series of *teas*, 'Tea to hammer Jewellery',
'Tea to talk Scandal', 'Tea to gather Gardenias', these
five-o'clocks of Bertie Waldorf were often notable affairs.

'Well, we'd better start right now, I reckon, 'fore the
fattest ones get pulled,' Mrs Rosemerchant astutely said,
attaching a large mauve-lipped orchid to her gown.

Between Riverside Park and Park Avenue Miss Hancock in otiose, blissful mood advanced but one observation: 'Your chauffeur, dear; the beautiful plant of his
neck, I love to see it!'

'Yes; necks, darling, tell me, too.'

Fearing nothing and amused by offering joy and

romance to rustic Loveliness, Mrs Rosemerchant, in guiding Miss Hancock's first social steps, found in her protégée a perfect type-foil.

'I want just to put you wise, dear child,' she fluted, applying a lip-stick to her long frail mouth, 'by saying that the house to which we're going is considered to be one of the wickedest in New York; Bertie, you must know, is horribly dangerous, and quite terribly rich — Cuba.'

'My brother Ben, the one I told you about, the illegitimate one, he went to Cuba!'

'Well, should Mr Waldorf ask you to Havana, or to his paradise near Matanzas, I needn't perhaps warn you to refuse.'

The bachelor-home of the young compiler of the *Glory-book of Complaisant Husbands* lay almost at the extremity of Upper Park Avenue. Planned from designs by Ronald Firbank, it possessed perhaps everything that a man might wish for except a garden.

The engrailed great gates opening invisibly to their ring, they were introduced to an atmosphere of studied unreality; reacting, somehow, upon the butler (who minced to meet them) in an oddly ludicrous way.

Climbing a dozen jasper steps, they crossed a broad hall, whose windows, masked by moucharabi, gave to New York without a piquant Far-Orient air.

'Where can be the beds, dear?' Miss Hancock wondered.

'What beds?'

'The strawberry-beds.'

Following on the domestic's heels, they were shown into a compartment with magenta and burnt-cream tinted walls, where a young man in tussore knickers and a

low-cut tan silk shirt appeared to be doing the honours.
Coming brightly forward, he greeted them with the news
that the master of the house was busy resting, after enter-
taining to lunch some impossibly insular English — Sir
Gigantic and Lady Emma Tulloch — and was now, in
consequence, busy suffering from an utter, utter weariness
in the arc of his throat.

'Say, though? But where are the beds, you?' Miss
Hancock simmered.

Gervaise Shymoon, the youth addressed, recoiled a
step. 'Well, I reckon the sleeping-apartments mostly are
on the floor above.'

'Oh, go on.'

'She means the fruit-beds, sure!'

'The strawberry fields? Why, I guess they're through
there.'

A sound of mandolines and nostalgic negro voices
lifted to some drowsy plantation air suggestive of harvest
crop-time and radiant noons, noons in azure Dixie or in
balmy Louisiana, reverberating faintly from the ballroom, seemed to indicate the way. Advancing through
shrouded flower-filled rooms, they had a vision of white
bending figures in large summer hats and loose swinging
strands of pearls, of gossiping, idling, fruiterers *à la mode*,
in a hundred natural (if unexpected) postures.

'Be sure to pinch me, Sweetie, if I eat too many.'

Rising here in terraced slopes, nestling there beneath
tall clumps of Indian palms and flame Flamboyants, growing in massed profusions everywhere, the brilliant blush-
ing fruit had usurped the finest dance-floor in town.

Seated amid the scarlet berries, the Duchess of Valdivia looking thrillingly pretty in a Greuze-like garden
gown was holding a small informal court.

'As if I mind any nice boy's fingers!' she was exclaiming, raising a gigantic ſtrawberry to her painted heart-shaped mouth.

Conversing brightly to right and left she professed herself charmed to be back.

'This year we think of letting our Newport villa and spending the summer somewhere on the sea-coast in France': a ſtaid pale woman with a peacock nose caught her volatile attention.

'You should try my pet plage, Vermillionville, if you do.'

'I have never heard of the place. Where is it?'

'Well, it's near Trouville and Deauville and all the other villes, and it's the laſt ville there is and the smarteſt and moſt expensive,' the Duchess with idyllic tenderness evoked it; 'and that's right where it is,' she added, turning about at a cry from Miss Joy Hoppin.

'O, a horrid frog, or something — it might have been a lizard.'

'Among those exotic ferns and grasses I should not be amazed at snakes,' the Duchess declared, absently opening her parasol.

From the trifling-type to the ſtrawberry-fiend, with fine shades between of ardour, the charaƈteriſtic tendencies of the gatherers might have proved, psychologically, an intereſting ſtudy; the propensity to *pounce* of Joshua Ward Junior was, beyond any doubt, decidedly hereditary; while the thrifty-hand, the hand that ſtrips, of Miss Prettyman-Price was to be accounted for equally too.

'The woman by the palm tree squatting: say did you ever see . . .' the Duchess tittered.

'Mrs. George Gogetit?'

'She apparently wears no under falals at all!'

'Well, and what of it? . . .' The query came from
C. Elihu Sanck, the inventor of Low Gowns for Boys.
An advocate for National dress, he had been arrested
more than once — on Broadway, and elsewhere — for a
Ku-Kluxer, while endeavouring to launch the mode of
lace-veils for men.

'Mon Dieu, what of it!' the Duchess murmured,
extending a free hand airily to Mrs Rosemerchant.

Hoisting her parasol in emulation of the Duchess, Miss
Hancock was made to feel by the instant falling of the
other that she had somehow gone too far.

'You'll find me, dear, about the beds,' she informed
her friend, strolling casually on.

Traversing an oasis exuberant with flaunting fan-palms
and rhododendrons of a quite new and amazing mauve,
Miss Hancock dropped daintily down among the busied
rows of gleaners.

Fastidious, selecting among the berries only the
soundest, the ripest, it was to be observed that she
deliberated each time before she picked.

'I guess you might be choosing a hat or something,'
Miss Joy Hoppin addressed her.

'A hat?'

'Or a husband!'

'Well, I like first testing.'

'I reckon you're right.'

'Holy gee! had I Mabelle Country's ankles, I'd choose
myself longer skirts,' a débutante with lilac eyes and a
pallid tongue declared, her regard ranging over the beds.

'I assure you they're not one half so droll as Florence
Fazakerley's!' Miss Hoppin rejoined, waving a gay-
daubed paper fan.

'Oh, Joy, dear, don't,' a young girl like a very worldly

mouse shook with laughter: 'no, don't,' she added, looking up at a pale youth who suggeſted Hamlet considering
a foot-squashed ſtrawberry.

Flitting along the beds, Miss Hancock reached a patch,
as yet praɛtically unravished, before which a couple of
dames were discussing a forthcoming divorce — an obſti-
nate wife, it seemed, that refused to reside on Jackson
Heights. . . . 'my dear, she swears nothing on God's
earth will make her mount there; she quite hates the
neighbourhood; the very notion of Jackson Heights
makes her dizzy!'

Sampling juſt as many berries as her aſtral number
(according to the horoscope of a Boſton Sibyl), Miss
Hancock sought a mossy bank beneath a palisade of
palms: such exquisite coolth . . . the ſtirring vernery . . .
how, by what art, was it managed? Turning, she espied
through the palm-fronds two small open glass doors
ajar.

Curiosity running away with discretion, Miss Hancock
rose: 'I guess I mean to track that draught,' she told herself, forcing a passage through the trembling boskage.

The forsaken corridor, with its sombre air of forbidden
charm, it was a perfeɛt joy to look down. Pursuing her
way along it, with the alert, self-conscious gait of a thief
on the movies, Miss Hancock paused to peep into a
chamber wholly devoid of chairs, the floor ſtrewn with
countless cushions in whose midſt was a harp with jade
ſtops and rose-red ſtrings.

'The scene of more than one orgy, I shouldn't wonder,'
she refleɛted, tempted to progress further.

Ascending some few ſteps she passed into the aloof
remoteness of an older time. So much beauty in decay
might have come right out of an English legend. The

tapestry-illumined walls, how strange they were and to
what could they allude? Here and there a unicorn fed
unconcernedly in a flowery field, or again a virgin passed
with neck bowed, absorbed in the perusal of an austere
missal, her sandalled feet very pale on the ice-blue grass.
And as if indeed to illustrate that Nature is eternal, such
Spring flowers as figured in the old, faded and historic
broideries were blossoming freshly in radiant counter-
part about the room.

'Why it's just like a fairy-tale,' she soliloquized,
glimpsing her face in a time-clouded mirror.

She was looking unreckonably temperamental in a
delicate mousseline dress, with a little veil, like a sea-net,
caught across the eyes.

'I guess here am I in the ogre's den!' she breathed,
lending a listening ear to someone singing — Farrar, or
Garden, was it? — to the company she had strayed from.

'I know a bank whereon the wild thyme blows,
Where oxlips and the nodding violet grows.'

'*A Midsummer Night's Dream* unless I'm mistaken,' she
smiled, her glance exploring a small but intriguing array
of books: *A Plea for the Separation of the Sexes.* A treatise
on *The Value of Smiles.* *Queens of the Rod and Birch.* The
Life and Times of Gaby Deslys. The *Holy Bible* (Authorized
Version). *Valmouth* — a presentation copy, it seemed,
from the author.

'Not a sign of the *Glory-book*!' she shrugged, turning
towards a flapping portière that seemed to indicate the
origin of the draught.

Lifting it she had the impression of a man 'busy resting'
upon a bedstead of flame-red lacquer.

'Gee!'

'Why, what the — ?'

Miss Hancock raised her eyes to the *Pietà* above the bed, the inspiration of some Renaissance artist-friar.

'I was but tracing the draught, sir,' she faltered.

VI

A sky like the darkest of cinerarias spread serenely above New York.

'Sweetie, dear, your arm.'

Leaving the ball betimes, both Flying-fox and Blue-bird (with a wing adroop) sought the grateful air: 'Any-where — Brooklyn Bridge — !' The chauffeur received instructions.

Delighting in a late spin, Mrs Rosemerchant was one of those who professed to find certain qualities, *influences*, in the mystic oxygen of the night not to be met with in the more candid, or less funeralized oxygen of the day; occult beneficial forces which would attain to their apotheosis towards the first flush of morning.

In an uplifted, though slightly stupefied condition, Miss Hancock was inclined to trace her symptoms to an etherized ice: 'I reckon the refreshments, sweetie, were some queer,' she observed, tucking a light rug be-sprinkled with iridescent moonstones about her knees.

'Not only; I should have said the whole *soirée*!'

'Strange how the men mostly seemed to go as humped cattle while the women all wore wings.'

Mrs Rosemerchant sighed ecstatically.

'*Our* sex,' she asserted, 'needs wings; what is a woman without wings?'

'There's the beautifullest song about wings! My brother

Ben, the one in the foot-troops, the illegitimate one, often
sings it.'

'Say, dearest, have you *no* legitimate relatives at all?'

'Several; but Dada, you see, he was inclined to be a
baby-making man.'

'Darling one, you're so cute. I sometimes think you
were born with rouge on both your cheeks,' Mrs Rosemerchant passed the observation.

'Well, anyway, it's just the beautifullest song.'

'Thrice perfect child, I'd give some to hear it.'

'It's called "Blue Pelican Land":

> *Won't you fly with me to Blue Pelican Land,*
> *To Blue Pelican Land —*

No. That's not it.

> *We'll fly away to Blue Pelican Land,*
> *To —*

I guess I forget it.'

Drowsing a little, she was inclined, Mrs Rosemerchant
fancied, to be under the soft enchantment of the ether
still.

They were passing along Broadway all poetized and
idealized by the night, whose dim, capricious buildings,
towering into the star-dust, suggested white shadowy
forms endeavouring (vainly) to escape from earth.

Miss Hancock surveyed somnolently the tranquil
firmament.

'It must be perfect over there, dear,' she murmured,
pointing with a cotillion favour at the moon: 'I guess I'm
crazy to visit it. Aren't you?'

'I dare say, darling, it's horribly boring,' Mrs Rosemerchant returned, taking the tinsel-glimmering object
from her hand.

Miss Hancock pensively considered it.

'All is not gold that — 'scuse me, dear, if I hiccupped — glitters; and that's very true! . . . Yes; as I was saying, sweetie, all that glitters is not gold; and the more's the pity!'

Mrs Rosemerchant dropped the bauble she was holding.

'For the Van Cottons to organize it certainly was a most unusual ball,' she commented.

'It somehow makes me smile, dear, to see a little weak man like that married to such a terrific, tremendous and terrifying person.'

'Small men like Otto, you know, admire big things. Just think of the Herc!'

'One would have thought his wife's own behind would have been sufficient.'

Mrs Rosemerchant glanced away, charmed by the heavy mauveness of the night.

They had reached Brooklyn Bridge, and the car had drawn up above the eager river's silver stretch.

'How too lyric, say.'

But Miss Hancock seemed disinclined to 'say' or to articulate any further.

'Then towards home;' the supple-necked Lionel had his orders.

Relaxing luxuriously her slender person, Mrs Rosemerchant gave herself up to thought. Her husband's growing jealousy of her so adorable friend, his objection to her, was exasperating.

'Really, he makes me mad,' she murmured, groping absently for a sack of bonbons beneath the rug.

They were on the long tree-shaded Avenue now; the one on which stands the stately gardened-about Convent

LADY FIRBANK
Ronald's mother, no date

following his wife, squeaking 'Vive America',
ambled the Duke of Valdivia.
"Freddy"

The Dancer Demetrias.   weeping & laughing.
Papa finds   falling hysterical
Herc laws kick." For a strong   "O, boy! It's 'some' behind

5 cent

on the packets ?

my portrait on Rosebuds Cigarette

Nicatini.

The pearl of the Golden Age —   flashing teeth & Than

"Herc".   off on a lorry   the New York
"naked men do my bean at home   thing
please me".   to break it on a trolley — not everyone
stiffly said.   Police object. null. "Say, wasn't Hercules the lover of Hel
Have you ever seen one?   Troy?"
Mrs Van Cotter plans

"It puts the Farnese Hercules to the wash — the duey

a line of limousines along the wharf —

                                        legs a Soda-Fountain
Victor d'ishu's   Champagne & strawberries rushed dow
Jazz. Demetrias the Greek dancer evoking "Alt
Pleasio   wild-sounding music — Recites from Iphegenia in A
ship sighted   raised arms of brass.   excerpts
off Sandy Hook —
    ten inches by eight? go on & tittery
    disturbing
    rumours held up on Ellis Island, neglect of formalities —
                    the mornings   "Pauline delos   Ellen
                    arresting transport   "I'm angelina   lambent light
chaptered in all. Greek Statue left in the heartiness by the sea — watchm
    Snowing long fingers marble one   glistening peach-toned marble
                    glistening   old god's beard.
                            nosey sharp & Sadie   (espionage)
                            Publicity agent & detecti

gers five by three, phallus ten by eight... an insane
was gratifying it had arrived intact be.   Then q the straclinter)
drifty   that all was as it should be.   Nice

"Gervaise" in white tussore

oddly dressed   ———

With her hair all in ringlets
& curleycues looking the image of her portrait on
                the image of early Mary Pickford –
       looking very small as mounted on the packet
       ——— of "Rosebud cigarettes –"

    a villa in the Valley of Yumuri,
Matanzas, Cuba

  "no, ta"
              ———

an obsession there was a Chinaman &
a brown man following her.

    ———

Rosemerchant finds Dreadfuline "ugly."
"Oh Harry, she's the sweetest looking
woman in the world" etc –
   Bankum & poppycock?"
"Oh, Harry!   ———

                                                    to greet ?
                                                    marble or
                                                    a guard

      Jo meet
  the arrival of the Hercules – dusk,
er New York Bay   perssmen
dawn, art – lovers waiting Praxitele
         purchased over the heads of english buyers of Bloom
masterpiece – resisted from the krone by the Alchemistry king's –
the – a tent by the wharf – Excitement   dawn time
                                                the opera –

RONALD FIRBANK
photographed by Bertram Park, 1917

of Joseph of Arimathea. Gone midnight, it was agreeable to evoke the slumbering sisterhood within contentedly dreaming of boy saints, mystic marriages and martyr-doms in China or elsewhere.

'Yes, we women want our wings, eh, darling?' Mrs Rosemerchant asked, taking seraphically in her own the hand loosely resting on the shining moonstones.

'Oh, sweetie Mrs Rosemerchant,' half-inaudibly Miss Hancock sighed.

VII

Flaunting a large striped tulip and swinging a cherry cane, Mrs Rosemerchant's small page, Co-co, set out one evening for the Negro Mission organized by the pious widow, Mrs Stella Mandarin Dove. He had arranged to pick up a coloured youth from Harlem before the public comfort station by Central Park, on the way to East Ninety-first Street together where the philanthropic widow lived.

A whitish twilight enveloped New York, and the Avenue lamps — shining away, and away — seemed to prance and dance as tho' running into Fairy-land: 'Sho', a Childs Dairy, or de door ob a church make a more select meetin'-place dan de one Posthumus gib me fo' now,' the niggerling brooded, scrambling dexterously to a Fifth-Avenue bus. Enthralled by all the movement of the streets, it was pleasant to forget awhile Cornelius the first footman, or Potter the butler, and the innumerable petty worries of life below stairs.

Descending near a fifty-five story clouds' rest in course of construction, he glimpsed his friend sauntering before the appointed spot. Exchanging brotherly greetings, they then directed their steps for the domicile of Mrs Dove.

The house on East Ninety-first Street, a frolicsome-looking pagan affair, seemed scarcely the setting best suited to such a benefactress of churchmen and churches as Mrs Stella Mandarin Dove. All ardour and zeal, notwithstanding her years, Mrs Dove was a woman who had been autrefois in the swim. Possessed of a considerable jointure (derived from something supposed to save 'Temper, Time and Money') she now devoted herself to the subduing of the senses, and to a soul-searching correspondence in the style of Christina of Pisa with certain prominent Princes of the Church.

With a birching match earlier in the afternoon, it had been for the matron a busy day. Clad in classic crêpe, her frail cheeks lashed with paint, she sought the retirement of an alcove with the Reverend Cedric Potts: 'I can never forgive him his treachery to the Archbishop of Trebizond,' she was saying with a look at the Bishop of London.

'No; or his attack on the late Cardinal Wiseman,' Father Potts complacently returned, considering a buxom negress.

Mrs Dove raised her gaze to a ceiling all over fans let into a vast white frame, then directed it on the room.

Already there was a goodly gathering. A number of pretty women who had assisted at the earlier function had lingered on in order to entertain the negroes, though no one was interesting them apparently more than a mere slip of a girl.

Exalted by her whipping to the last point of gaiety, she was giving out trill after trill of light, happy, irresponsible laughter.

'I was rather afraid for her; but she took her first punishment well,' the widow murmured.

'You were not, I surmise, too severe!'

'The thorny twigs of her birching bouquet were softened by a few premature chrysanthemums,' Mrs Dove returned in sweet firm tones, turning to greet Bertie Waldorf.

From his studiously simple dress, he looked as though he might be out for Chinatown, or off to Fairbanks in Alaska.

'I thought I'd look in early before the Mission-prayers begin,' he breathed, bending to kiss the widow's hand.

'You are not to desert us; I depend on you, you know, to edify the League!' Mrs Dove declared.

'Well; I guess I shall do my triple utmost,' he returned, observing in the offing a negro lad, in the fruit-packing line, with whom he had a slight previous acquaintance. Struck by his Gauguinish grace, he crossed the room to where he was standing.

'I want to paint you *nu*.'

'New?'

'Yes, *nu*; will you pose to me?'

. . .

THE NEW RYTHUM

Extracts from the Notebooks

For finale tutto? suggestion

The complete disappearance of Mrs Rosemerchant and of her young friend from the American scene made a profound sensation. Press and police investigations failed. Rumours from time to time reached New York that they had been seen together in Paris restaurants or in Egypt. While some believed they were living together in the mountains of Nirvana — in those blue hills. Many, and particularly Mr Rosemerchant's friends, believed that he had quietly murdered them.

N.B. preceding chapter should be poetic lyric fantastic anything. Then cold snap as —

---

*Notes**

the bishop, looking in a mood to buck the tiger
her laugh a frail white screech — for Negress?
African Golf
cats' pyjamas
a flowered grip-sack

nine
800

knew by heart the names of the 600 churches in New York
which she would recite on request in jazz-like tones
reached the *B's*:
St Benedict the Moor's —   tunefully
Bethel
faithful to Brick Church
Broadway Tabernacle
her white hair and dog-rose colouring
her long shrinking line
her frail cheeks lashed with paint

*Original spellings retained.

'I want to paint you *nu.*'   to Grab Thomson?
                                     the young Negro light-
                                     weight champion?

raised her long violet arms —   (negress
'Who, oh, who could hold a candle to him.'
'Insatiable spirit!'
recourseful —

Mrs D
raised indignant eyes to a ceiling all over fans let into a
vast white frame
Evangeline
heavy sated eyes
a large woman of entrancing fairness
    said, protruding his tongue, a dark washed rose
    shewed his tongue — a dark washed rose
    charmed by his tongue a dark washed rose
low rich Negro laughter
turned aside to lend an ear to Bertie Waldorf
extending hopes to a knot of negresses of a Riviera-
existence in Paradise
took her first punishment well
getting more and more light-headed — indeed, up-
roareous (Mabelle)
Theories on Twilight sleep
a negro who seemed to be counting the buttons on the
Bishop of London's leggings. 'I count dem three times,
an' *ebery* time dey come different!'
blossomed into smiles
Elaline Duplex-Taylor's card-lilies
Hairpin Ring = Wyllis Fusell?

Co-co and Mrs White the Negress
Mrs Isaac Cornabilt's 'gift'
Cornelius

Luna Park
shapely in a blue Store suit
sauntering before the public comfort station
an aversion for the subway
a pallid face, and the tremendous tired eyes of a Cassandra
trailing her widow's trappings
coloured youth
ball room manners
                                        a closed
a negro and a white woman dancing discreetly to the
gramaphone-strains of Yalula la Yalula
'Goose breens!'
a flower it give a finishment so nice
a satisfaxshun
'cos I'se a lil ahine-hand wid polishin' de cuspidors
a tiahd-like look under de eye
proud an' kintemphis
fond ob feddehs
way down Souf
he seem a man ob chahm
an' he in de spurrit world
the iris negresses
smeared with an ointment ob greenish crocodile's fat

murmured, making wistful eyes
a long, meagre coon
a negress of great size   Mrs Cash?
'Oh me good sah'
y'u
glanced at her big silver shoe-buckles
a gay taste in neckties
'I tell him to suck his teeth'
'Ah, sir, I have deceived my husband!'

'What made you do that?' The Bishop could think of
nothing better to say
digging phantom yam-holes with a hoe
I run 'Cosy Tea-Shop'
Celestina
I am satisfy
de Ole Buoy = devil
he come home to me wunst a munt
a married ooman
a pahty dat licketty-switch
a glass ob red currend wine
'Chooh, nebba!'
de hubsom ob a frien'
I pray every day that the Lord will change me white!
You're just as well as you are Mrs Storykoff. Stay black,
my dear, you might do worse.

A Miscellany

H

A MISCELLANY OF SHORT PASSAGES
FROM UNPUBLISHED WRITINGS

From a fragment of a short story written at the age of about twelve:

Mrs Keston put the dog in its basket, tidid her hair before a mirror, langwidley sat down and calved a chicken.

[A girl at a boarding school told to eat up the under-done beef she had left on her plate replies:]
'I have quite enough blood in my family without going to a bullock for more.'

Mr White-Morgan the Diamond King

(aged about fourteen)

[Mr White-Morgan has bought a large tract of Soho, pulled down the buildings and built himself a house with a huge garden, where he is giving a party to which Lady Violet Wilmington and her daughter Ethel have been invited. Ethel is looking forward to enjoying the country air:]
'If you call Old Cumpton [*sic*] Street country air, my poor child!' murmured her mother.
'It will be quite country enough for me, besides the

real country bores me so, I am only fond of the country when I see it on the stage.'

Impression d'Automne—A Poem in Prose[1]

Surely at the foot of the trees that they once made green, which now in the misty air rise like skeletons from the sodden earth, the leaves are lying as though in Purgatory, waiting for the wind to scatter them to the North, to the South, to the East, to the West, as ships are scattered on the sea by the storm.

Alas, where now the daffodil? Where now the violet? Then, in that happy time, they did not think it wonderful to feel the first hot kiss of the morning sun, or receive the cooling silver of the evening moon.

The Widow's Love

Mrs Fawley [a widow who 'loved looking at herself in a crisis'] had only twelve expressions, she wanted so much to have another.

'Nothing shall induce me to go into mauve,' she said, 'I shall be quite brave and live only for my dressmaker and for my garden.'

Her week-ends were a noted success. She arranged a circle of deck-chairs under the lime trees on her lawn,

[1] Published as 'Souvenir d'Automne' in *Supplement to The King and his Navy and his Army*, 2nd December 1905.

and everyone slept. It was so restful, her friends said, and then when one could not sleep one could always talk scandal to one's neighbour, with one's eyes closed.

[Mrs van Cotton] a stout little American dressed in yellow and gold. She reminded one vaguely of a restaurant ceiling. She had her portrait in the Academy, which was mistaken by the public for a sunset.

The Mauve Tower

(A dream play in seven scenes)

[*The Princess* INGRIA *and her slave* LIERIES *have wandered from her home and in due course reach the Mauve Tower, where the young Sultan is virtually imprisoned. The princess wears a robe of blue-green gauze embroidered with silver flowers. In her hair black and white ostrich feathers are fastened to a pale red veil. Her hair falls to her feet and is plaited with rubies and strange mauve stones. As she walks the stones jingle and her veil floats behind her like a sail.*]

LIERIES I see strange pictures in the moon.

INGRIA What do you see?

LIERIES I am afraid.

INGRIA The sea looks like a yellow fire, like a sheet of yellow flame . . . listen! how still it is . . . the birds have ceased to sing. . . . All the palm trees are trembling, and yet there is no wind. Never before have I felt a night so hot. Oh! how dark it is, I cannot see the flowers, I can no longer see the moon. Lieries, Lieries, I cannot see you. Oh! Oh! I am afraid.

LIERIES	Something terrible is going to happen
INGRIA	Where are we? Where can we be?
LIERIES	I do not know. *Curtain. Music plays softly.*

[*The sentry has refused them admission to the Tower.*]

LIERIES	Let us be gone, let us be gone.
INGRIA	No, I will not go, I wish to see the Sultan.
LIERIES	Why do you wish to see the Sultan?
INGRIA	I do not know.

LAON	Oh how beautiful your eyes are when they cloud with tears. Your eyes are like two blue flowers, two blue flowers after rain.
INGRIA	Oh! how sweet your voice sounds when you speak. It is like a distant harp, it sounds like a harp, played far away upon a sea-shore.

LAON	Why, why were you afraid?
INGRIA	I do not know. (*A silence*) Why did you pursue us with a sword?
LAON	I do not know.
INGRIA	We know nothing. (*A silence*)

A Tragedy in Green

(Dedicated: 'To the Inspirer of the Tragedy,
Sir Coleridge Kennard')

'I am a work of art,' she [Lady Georgia Blueharnis] sighed, 'and this evening I feel nearly as wicked as Herodias.' It was one of Lady Georgia's habits to find equivalents for all her worser feelings in the Bible.

. . . the sort of woman who will play Debussy before

lunch when every village child knows that he should only be listened to by electric light.

. . . a Turkish periodical, with a gorgeous supplement of a massacre, printed in two colours — red and blue.

'Green!' she [Lady Georgia] cried lyrically, 'colour — mine! I don't care about you in trees, nor do I like you in vineyards, or meadows, and least of all at sea! But in *rooms*, in *carpets*, in *brocades*, and oh! in gowns, you are the only colour that brings to me content.'

True Love

[Alwyn St Claire, the poet.] His long pale face was surrounded in an aureole of wavey golden hair, and his big blue eyes and bright red lips contrasted vividly with his pale complexion. He looked aesthetic. He was well, but rather curiously dressed, his waistcoat was of black and silver brocade.

[Miranda.] A beautiful woman in black was standing in the open window, over her left shoulder fell a great feather boa, and in her hands she held a quantity of blue and white violets. She was very thin and looked pale; her face was half hidden under the long lace veil that fell from her hat. On the front of her dark gown was fastened a large diamond cross; she wore no other jewels.

She crossed the room to where the great silver crucifix stood and all through the long long night she prayed for him. . . .

A Disciple from the Country

(A one-act play)

[MRS CREAMWAY, a rich Australian widow, is launching her daughter STELLA in London Society with the help of LADY SEAFAIRER, a paid chaperone. STELLA's 'line' is to be ultra-*dévote*, in consequence of which she is known in Society as 'Saint Angelica'. LORD BLUEHARNIS is her suitor. MRS BLOSSOME, described as 'an uneducated person who still believes in miracles', has heard about STELLA's sanctity and walked all the way from her home in Warwickshire (where she owns a piggery) to London in order to be healed of her ailments by the Saint.]

LADY SEAFAIRER   The last girl I chaperoned — a Miss Gosford — took me four summers and a winter in Cairo. Happily she is married to one of Lord Cotswold's boys now. . . .

. . . One evening she came in from riding in the sun and fainted. I never saw her look prettier; fainting suited her. 'Do it again,' I said, 'do it again,' and she did it most beautifully. That evening at the Opera we had stalls, just under the State Box. I always maintain that stalls are more advantageous for an unmarried girl. In a Box you may come and go unnoticed without disturbing a soul, but in the

Stalls it is different. Well! just as Wotan was beginning to get the least bit wearisome Miss Gosford *swooned*. I was totally unprepared. Music seems to sap all the strength out of me. I just turned and looked at her. She was leaning to the left on the arm of a most distinguished-looking personage, looking, I am bound to say, perfectly charming. At that moment a slight tap on the right shoulder brought me to my senses. I looked up . . . I shivered . . . The Queen was handing me a glass of brandy and water!

STELLA   And did Miss Gosford marry the distinguished-looking personage?

LADY SEAFAIRER   (*Mysteriously*) He was the father. It was Lord Cotswold.

LADY SEAFAIRER   . . . people already talk of her as Saint Angelica, it will be her own fault if she doesn't marry *at least* a Bishop. (*Confidentially*) There are no fewer than fourteen single Bishops in England at this present moment, Mrs Creamway. Thirteen of them are widowers. Stella is artistic, in a Cathedral she would find scope for her tastes. Erecting a window to herself here, altering the position of a pulpit there, resting in the sanctuary when

she felt tired, making daisy-chains
for the dear Bishop as the Calendar
decrees . . .

STELLA   I believe you are in love with a Bishop
yourself, Lady Seafairer.

LADY SEAFAIRER   (*Poetically*) I am in love with a certain
Cathedral that I know.

MRS CREAMWAY   . . . Providentially I happened to pass
by in the lift at that moment, laden
with my curios — my morning's shop-
ping. I had some Venetian lace, I
remember, and a Papal throne.

LADY SEAFAIRER   . . . like most of the world's attractive
saints, she has a sympathetic know-
ledge of life's little foibles, and unlike
them, she always manages to be perfectly dressed. I predict for her a
radiant future, at all events in *this*
world.

STELLA   [*Apropos of a lady of whom it had been
said that she 'suggested sheep'*] 'Zhink
of the numbers and numbers of people
who suggest nothing whatever, my
dear,' she said to me when I told her,
'and besides it is nice to look as
though one owned sheep, people will
think I have a place in the country.'

MRS CREAMWAY [*Alluding to* STELLA] Dear child, she has a passion for books that one cannot obtain everywhere. Only yesterday I spent most of my morning hunting for a pamphlet which satisfactorily proves that Mary Magdalen was actually engaged to John the Baptist. It was only after the sad affair at the Palace that Mary really buckled to and became what she afterwards became. They tell me the whole thing has been turned quite recently into a very tuneful opera. In these days nobody seems safe from being set to music . . .

. . . She is in many ways a mystic — I have it from her maid, who should certainly know.

LORD BLUEHARNIS . . . I had always thought of your daughter as exceptionally hardy.

MRS CREAMWAY Hardy! What a dreadful expression! I would sooner see Stella indisposed than hardy. Hardy girls are generally forward, and invariably sly. In my opinion the child is relaxed, run down. When a girl is fond of Gregorian music there is generally something wrong.

MRS CREAMWAY No really nice woman would walk all the way from Warwickshire.

Mrs Blossome	Oh the sweet young lamb, at last I sees you! (*Stroking the hem of* Stella's *frock*) Oh! the clean white robe! Washed by angels, I can see. No laundry ever scrubbed them frillies — done in Heaven to the sound of harps.
Stella	How clever of you to have guessed. A French Nun made me this. She is starting a millinery establishment of her own in the Avenue Malakoff.
Mrs Creamway	(*Enlighteningly*) Just off the Elysian Fields. I daren't say it in French.
Mrs. Blossome	The Elesian Fields! Where the saints sit all day on garden seats and warm their hands in the sun?
Mrs Creamway	Quite close. In front of one of the Embassies, I have forgotten which, the third floor, but fortunately there's a lift. You cannot mistake the place, besides, 'Aux Anges Elégants' is written in Gothic characters across the door.
Stella	There's generally a violin going and some tea. Then, afterwards, when the incense that is always kept burning before the prettiest gowns has gone a little to one's head and one is feeling thoroughly amiable and extravagant, Mademoiselle Gabrielle appears and tempts one with a fur wrap or a Renaissance fan.
Mrs Blossome	The wicked hussy! But we need only

open the Bible to see how the Saints
was always sorely tried.

LORD BLUEHARNIS As a Saint's mother, what do you
consider the right sort, Mrs Cream-
way?

MRS CREAMWAY (*With great decision*) A person with a
permanent Opera Box, Lord Blue-
harnis, and a habitable fortress in the
North.

LORD BLUEHARNIS I'm afraid with such ideals you could
never look with indulgence on a
simple cottage in Surrey.

MRS CREAMWAY A great deal would depend on the
landlord. A well-born man is capable
of redeeming his surroundings, be
they what they may.

LORD BLUEHARNIS I wish my little cottage could hear
you say so. Unfortunately it has no
idea of being redeemed, or it might
find a means of closing its hospitality
to rats.

MRS CREAMWAY (*In a tone of voice she would use to an
invalid not expected to recover*) Rats! My
poor friend! . . . (*then with forced cheer-
fulness*) I can tell you of some wonderful traps that only require half the
usual amount of cheese.

STELLA . . . the black Tuscan straw hat I wore
at Ascot, with cascades of blue and

pink wisteria came from 'Claude' of
the Rue de la Paix. Mr Waterbury, the
owner of Sulky Max, said his horse's
miraculous win was due to me. Immediately the animal perceived my
wisteria nodding in the wind, it became perfectly possessed and *flew*. It
was a most gratifying advertisement
to Madame Claude, who immediately
deducted off my account the cost of
the trimmings. I think with absolute
confidence you may predict to your
readers [of the *Smart World*] that, for
the race-course in future, Wisteria
will be the flower à la mode.

APPENDIX

The Manuscripts and Correspondence of
Arthur Annesley Ronald Firbank (1886–1926)
Offered for Sale by Sotheby & Co.
on Tuesday, December 12, 1961

A. AUTOGRAPH MANUSCRIPTS

The spelling throughout is as in the originals

1 Fragment of a short story, autograph manuscript,
2 *pp.*, *4to* [*c.* 1898]; Lay of the Last Nurserymaid, 1 *page, two five-line stanzas*, autograph manuscript, *in pencil, beginning:*
> The hand was raised,
> The child was there!

and ending:
> The mother stood irate from top to toe
> Her eyes spoke volumes, doom and woe.

2 Mr White-Morgan the Diamond King, autograph
manuscript, 12 *pp.* 8vo (*unfinished*), *corrected in pencil and* (*at a much later date*) *in purple ink on paper headed 'The Coopers, Chislehurst'*
[*c.* 1900]

3 The Wind and The Roses (To be set to Music), autograph
manuscript, *forty-three line poem*, 2 *pp.*, *folio*, unpublished [*c.* 1902]

4 The Roses were never called before seven . . . , auto-
graph manuscript, 5 *pp.* folio, *with revisions and corrections* [*c.* 1902]

5 La Princesse aux Soleils, autograph manuscript, *cover*

and 10 *leaves on stiff paper, written in red, blue, purple, yellow and green ink, partly on one side of the leaf only,* DECORATED BY THE AUTHOR, *held together by multiple coloured ribbons*

4to (10 *in. by* 8 *in.*) [*Paris*], 1904

6 FAR AWAY, AUTOGRAPH MANUSCRIPT, 8 *pp.* 8vo, *written on paper headed 'The Coopers, Chislehurst'* Paris, 24 *July* 1904

7 LA PRINCESSE AUX SOLEILS, AUTOGRAPH MANUSCRIPT, *covers and* 4 *ll., on thick paper, written in black ink on both sides, French text only, inscribed 'A ma soeur adorée j'envoie la deuxième edition de mon livre. Artie.* 5 *Septembre* 1904*', the upper cover decorated with a water-colour drawing of the Princess, held together by twisted gold thread*

8vo (7¼ *in. by* 4½ *in.*) [*Paris*], 5 *Septembre* 1904

8 IDEAS AND FANCIES, AUTOGRAPH MANUSCRIPT, *covers and* 10 *ll., on thick paper, partly on one side only, interleaved with leaves of gold gauze to which have been stuck 'petals' of rose-coloured silk,* DECORATED BY THE AUTHOR THROUGHOUT, *held together by multiple coloured ribbons hung with bells* 8vo (9 *in. by* 5 *in.*) *Paris,* [*December*] 1904

9 REVERIE and FLAVIA, AUTOGRAPH MANUSCRIPT, *in French, in a notebook,* 8½ *pp.* 4to, *corrected in pencil,* UNPUBLISHED [*c.* 1904]

10 PREFACE TO THE AMERICAN EDITION OF 'THE FLOWER BENEATH THE FOOT', AUTOGRAPH DRAFT, 4 *pp.* 4to, *in purple ink, heavily corrected and with alternative copies of the first page* [1924]

11 Autograph rough notes for novels or short stories, *on six scraps of paper, one dated* 27 *April* 1925; 'I do not in the least judge people by their shoes,' etc.

12 [THE NEW RYTHUM], AUTOGRAPH MANUSCRIPT, FIRST DRAFT EXTENSIVELY REVISED BY THE AUTHOR, 62 ll. folio, comprising Chapters 1–6 and part of Chapter 7 (all that was completed) and 4 pp. of notes, *unbound* [1925–26]

13 THE NEW RYTHUM, AUTOGRAPH MANUSCRIPT, *a fair copy of*

Chapters 1–6 *incorporating the revisions in the first draft, in a 4to note-book,* 54 *pp., written in purple ink, blue cloth covers*   [1925–26]

B. TYPESCRIPTS

14   THE MAUVE TOWER, A Dream Play in VII Scenes, *typescript, title, dedication, list of characters and scenes and* 24 *pp. folio, green wrappers, inscribed by the author on the title 'Not to publish!'*   [1904]

15   ODETTE D'ANTREVERNES, *typescript, title and* 12 *pp. folio, green wrappers*   [1904]

16   IMPRESSION D'AUTOMNE. A Poem in Prose, *typescript, title and* 2 *pp, folio, dated at end* 7 *October* 1905, *green wrappers the same as No* 39, *except for the title*

17   THE LEGEND OF SAINT GABRIELLE, *typescript, title and* 4 *pp. folio, one correction on p.* 4, *inscribed by the author on title 'Not to be published. RF.', grey wrappers,* UNPUBLISHED   *no date*

18   TRUE LOVE, *typescript, title and* 9 *pp. folio, inscribed by the author on title 'Not to Publish R.F', green wrappers,* UNPUBLISHED
no date

19   TRUE LOVE, *another copy of the typescript, uninscribed*

20   THE SINGING BIRD AND THE MOON, *typescript, title and* 8 *pp. folio, inscribed by the author on the title 'Not to be published RF,' green wrappers,* UNPUBLISHED   *no date*

21   HER DEAREST FRIEND, *typescript, title and* 8 *pp. folio, one correction on p.* 1, *title inscribed by the author 'Not to be published,' green wrappers,* UNPUBLISHED   *no date*

22   A TRAGEDY IN GREEN, *typescript, no title, dedication leaf to Sir Coleridge Kennard inscribed by the author 'Not to be published RF,' and* 18 *pp. 4to, with autograph corrections, and rewritings, dark green wrappers,* UNPUBLISHED   *no date*

23 LADY APPLEDORE'S MÉSALLIANCE. An Artificial Pastoral, *title and 40 pp. 4to, a few autograph corrections and additions, inscribed by the author on the title '? Revise considerably in places — If — ,' dark green wrappers, stamp on last leaf of a typewriting bureau at Cambridge*

no date

24 THE WIDOW'S LOVE, *typescript, title and 10 pp. folio, inscribed by the author on the title 'Not to be published RF,' grey wrappers,* UN-PUBLISHED *no date*

25 THE ARTIFICIAL PRINCESS, *typescript, 82 pp. 4to, no title, autograph corrections on p. 62, grey wrappers* *no date*

26 A DISCIPLE FROM THE COUNTRY [a one-act play], *typescript, leaf with list of characters and 35 pp. 4to, no title, lacks upper wrapper, inscribed by the author on first page 'Not to be published,' grey lower wrapper,* UNPUBLISHED *no date*

27 INCLINATIONS. Chapter IV. Part II, 11 *pp. 4to, dated at end* 'Rome April 1925'. *This revised version was printed alongside the original in* THE COLLECTED WORKS OF RONALD FIRBANK (*limited edition,* 1929) *Volume II, pp. 133–141*

C. AUTOGRAPH NOTEBOOKS

28 MISCELLANEOUS AUTOGRAPH NOTEBOOK, containing at the end some notes for *Vainglory,* 60 *ll., written on both sides in black ink and pencil, unbound, leaves loose* 12*mo* [*c.* 1914]

29 VAINGLORY, 15 AUTOGRAPH NOTEBOOKS, 803 *ll., written on both sides, mostly in black ink but in parts in pencil, red or purple ink, two unbound, one notebook has the ticket of Warrington and Co., 23 Garrick St., London, W.C.* 8*vo and smaller* [*c.* 1914]

30 INCLINATIONS, 10 AUTOGRAPH NOTEBOOKS, 591 *ll., written on both sides, almost entirely in black ink, one unbound, one notebook has*

the ticket of W. and C. Lane, 25 Southampton Row and 1 Sicilian Avenue,
W.C., one notebook with a pencil drawing of a woman at the beginning
8vo (not uniform) [c. 1915]

31 CAPRICE, 4 AUTOGRAPH NOTEBOOKS, 310 *ll., written on both*
sides, in black ink, two are stamped 'William Hunt, 18 Broad St., Oxford'
8vo [c. 1916]

32 VALMOUTH, 7 AUTOGRAPH NOTEBOOKS, 440 *ll., written on*
both sides, mostly in black ink but sometimes in pencil, LAVISHLY ILLUS-
TRATED THROUGHOUT *with very amusing pen-and-ink or pencil sketches,*
mostly of scenes or portraits for the novel, one notebook only half full and
containing notes for 'Valmouth' on a loose leaf, one unbound, four are
stamped 'William Hunt, 18 Broad St., Oxford'
4to, 8vo and smaller [c. 1917–19]

33 PRINCESS ZOUBAROFF, 2 AUTOGRAPH NOTEBOOKS, 121 *ll.,*
written on both sides in black ink and pencil, one notebook stamped 'William
Hunt, 18 Broad St., Oxford' *8vo (not uniform) [c. 1919]*

34 SANTAL, ONE AUTOGRAPH NOTEBOOK, 40 *ll., written on both*
sides in black ink, with some amendments in blue or purple ink, stiff blue
wrappers, the upper cover stamped 'Burdigala' *12mo [1920–21]*

35 THE FLOWER BENEATH THE FOOT, 5 AUTOGRAPH NOTE-
BOOKS, one of which also contains notes for *Santal,* 230 *ll., one*
notebook written on one side of the leaves, the others on both sides, the earliest
(that containing the notes for 'Santal') written in black and blue ink, the
others in purple ink, upper cover of one notebook lacking, another bound in
stiff green flowered wrappers *sm. 4to and smaller [c. 1920–21]*

36 PRANCING NIGGER (published in England under the title
Sorrow in Sunlight), 3 AUTOGRAPH NOTEBOOKS *and an envelope, post-*
marked 4 February 1924, with two notes for the novel on the back, 172 ll.,
mostly written on one side only, in purple ink *sm. 8vo [1922–24]*

37 CONCERNING THE ECCENTRICITIES OF CARDINAL PIRELLI,
4 AUTOGRAPH NOTEBOOKS, one containing notes for The New Rythum,

253 ll., written, mostly on one side only, in purple ink, one notebook has the ticket of 'E. Calzone, Roma,' another is stamped 'Warrington and Co., 22 Garrick Street, W.C.1' 4to and 8vo [1923–25]

38 THE NEW RYTHUM, 2 AUTOGRAPH NOTEBOOKS, 178 *ll.*, *written on one side only in purple ink, 5 ll. of notes loosely inserted, one on writing-paper of Shepheard's Hotel, Cairo*

sm. 8vo (*not uniform*) [1925–26]

D. PRINTED BOOKS

39 THE FAIRIES WOOD, *poem of five four-line stanzas, signed A.F.* (*Arthur Firbank*) *at the foot, printed on a card, verso blank* (4½ in. by 3½ in.), *n.d.* [*c.* 1904]. — Souvenir d'Automne. A Poem in Prose. By Arthur Annesley Ronald Firbank, *one page, with decoration, two copies* (*both slightly defective*), *folio,* Supplement to The King and his Navy and Army, Dec. 2nd, 1905

40 ODETTE, *second edition, trial copy* (?) *bound in white cloth, title and author's name stamped in gold on the upper cover, without the illustrations, loosely inserted is a page from the proof of the first edition* (1905) *and a coloured reproduction of Charles Shannon's portrait of Firbank,* Grant Richards, 1916; with an ordinary copy of the second edition, *four illustrations after Albert Buhrer, decorated wrappers,* 1916   8vo (2)

41 VAINGLORY, *second* (*first American*) *edition, coloured frontispiece after Félicien Rops, original black cloth, lettered in gilt on upper cover and spine, in dust-wrapper which has a coloured illustration after Joseph Fannell, two copies*   8vo New York, Brentano's, [1925] (2)

E. LETTERS FROM RONALD FIRBANK

42 A HIGHLY IMPORTANT SERIES OF 310 A. Ls. s. (*two imperfect*) AND TWO INSCRIBED CARDS TO HIS MOTHER, LADY FIRBANK ('Baba') 1897–1924, *many with envelopes, with a childish drawing* (1897) *by Ronald*

APPENDIX

Firbank inscribed to his mother and an autograph draft letter of Lady Firbank to Sir Joseph Duveen

*** In date the letters are as follows: 1898–1906, three letters and one card; 1912–14, twenty-nine letters and one card; 1915–19, eight letters (one imperfect); 1920, forty-four letters (one imperfect); 1921, eighty-four letters; 1922, sixty-nine letters; 1923, seventy-two letters; 1924, one letter.

43 FINE SERIES OF 42 A. Ls. s. TO HIS SISTER, HEATHER, *Cambridge, Berlin, Oxford, London, Cassis, Tunis, Venice, Versailles, Fiesole, Bordighera, Rome, Arcachon and Helwan, 1898–1926, most with envelopes*

44 COLLECTION OF 456 PICTURE POSTCARDS TO HIS SISTER, HEATHER, 1907–15 and 1921–23, *Kingston (Jamaica), Bermuda, Ghent, Brussels, Florence, Bruges, Rome, Taormina, Naples, Siena, San Gimignano, Chartres, Lisbon, Cairo, Vienna, Salzburg, Munich, Dresden, Berlin, Bath, Salisbury, York, Amiens, Bourges, Orléans, Assisi, Stratford, Oxford, Versailles, Vévey, Montreux, Fiesole, Santiago de Cuba, Myrtle Bay (Jamaica), Bordighera, etc.,* with autograph addresses, the majority with no text but some with short text, usually in French before 1914; with three P. Cs. from Ronald Firbank to his mother and a quantity of P. Cs. to Heather Firbank from other correspondents. *(a parcel)*

45 A. L. s. (draft of copy), 1 *p.* 8*vo, Hotel Bristol, Bordighera, 20 November* 1922, [to Messrs. Field Garner of Bond St.], disputing an account: 'no authorization was given to take speculators to Newport at my expense'

46 FINE A. L. (marked 'Copy'), 3½ *pp.* 8*vo, Villa Olivetti, Bordighera, 18 June* 1923, to his publisher, Grant Richards; he finished his book [*Sorrow in Sunlight*] yesterday; goes on to question the correctness of Grant Richards's latest statement of account; 'I find since 1914 I have spent not far short of £1,000 on the productions of my books'; points out that in New York his novels fetch high prices and encloses a priced list issued by Blanche W. Knopf

APPENDIX

47   A. L. s., 2 *pp.* *8vo*, 36 *Via Porta Pinciana, Rome*, 21 *February* 1925, to Hallett (Lady Firbank's maid), declining her suggestion that he should return to England as he has finished his book [*Cardinal Pirelli*]; with a copy of Hallett's letter to which this is a reply, and a covering letter from Hallett to Heather Firbank   (3)

48   A. L. s., 1 *p.* *4to, Hotel Quirinale* [*Rome*], *n.d.* [*May* 1926?], to 'Mr. Edouard', apologizing for not being up when his correspondent called and refusing his flat as he has found no suitable servant.

***   Probably Ronald Firbank's last letter, left unposted at his death, which occurred in the Hotel Quirinale on 21 May 1926. He had returned from wintering in Egypt and, in accordance with his usual practice, was no doubt looking for a quiet flat in which to finish his current novel, *The New Rythum.*

F. LETTERS TO RONALD FIRBANK
Omitted here

G.   MISCELLANEOUS

61   Documents relating to Ronald Firbank's education, including school list of Mortimer Vicarage School, June 1896, testimonials from his various tutors in France, England and Spain, 1901–06, and 3 A. Ls. s. from G. B. Shirres, his tutor at Cambridge, 1906   (15)

62   Certificate of discharge from the Army after one day's service, *Oxford*, 11 *June* 1917; visiting card, copy (in his mother's hand, with corrections) of his entry in Kelly's Handbook, 2 A. Ls. s. from Lady Firbank to Heather Firbank, both mentioning Ronald Firbank, and various miscellaneous documents; a copy of his will; copies of correspondence with Heather Firbank relating to his burial in Rome, showing that (contrary to Lord Berners's account) his remains were removed to the Catholic cemetery at Verano, etc.
      (*a parcel*)

APPENDIX

63   Book of Common Prayer, *coloured title and frontispiece, inscribed* '*Arthur Ronald Firbank from his affectionate Godmother May Staple-ton/March* 1886,' *brown morocco, g.e., Sacred Monogram in coloured enamel on the upper cover, by Field,* 65 *Regent St.*   12*mo Oxford, no date.*

64   Firbank family album, containing press-cuttings, etc., and, loosely inserted, seven photographs of Ronald Firbank (one signed and dated 1905) and two of his rooms at Trinity Hall, 1907, *brown morocco gilt by T. Chapman, large* 4*to*; and a large quantity of press-cuttings relating to Ronald Firbank's books, many marked by him.

65   Nevinson (C.R.W.) The original drawing for the endpapers of *Prancing Nigger, pen-and-ink on card, signed and dated* 1924   (5 *in. by* 4 *in.*)

The Complete
Ronald Firbank

contains *Odette*, *The Artificial Princess*, *Vainglory*, *Inclinations*, *Caprice*, *Valmouth*, *Santal*, *The Flower Beneath the Foot*, *Prancing Nigger*, *Concerning the Eccentricities of Cardinal Pirelli* and *The Princess Zoubaroff*. With an introduction by Anthony Powell, and photo frontispiece.

'The voice is unmistakable. Never rising above a whisper, it has triumphed over all the loud and important clamour of its time. Firbank is one of the few writers of this century who is certain to survive it, if anything does.'

Listener

'His books are not foolish trifles scribbled down to get through the boredoms of a languid and luxurious life. They are extremely intellectual and composed with the closest attention: dense textures of indirection that always disguise point. They have to be read with care, and they can be read again and again.' EDMUND WILSON—*New Yorker*

'It is an art which we look at through a frame; which we listen to as if a quartet were playing a long way off in a great concert hall. But when we look up from the picture, when we listen again to the noises of the street, what we see and hear has been a little changed by our deliberate experience of the picture and the music.' PHILIP TOYNBEE—*Observer*

Black buckram gilt.   766 *pages.*   42*s. net*